Y0-ARY-784

Short Stories by Texas Authors

A Collection of
Award-Winning Stories
Vol. 3

Published by Texas Authors, Inc.

Copyright © 2017

All rights reserved. Neither this book, nor any parts within it may be sold or reproduced in any form without permission.

ISBN: 978-0-9967348-2-0

Printed in the United States of America

CONTENTS

PASSAGE

Sandra Fox Murphy

O PAL CLIMBED, STEP by step, onto the Trailways bus that appeared to consume each passenger as if it were an ancient whale in the Mediterranean Sea. The late morning air in Palestine wilted the essence of the cottonwoods in summer's brutal humidity of east Texas. Opal wore her cotton shirtwaister, the one she had bought at the Grand Leader department store, the one with the pink flowers all over. It was her favorite, having softened over the years with each washing. Her hair's errant curls were peppered with gray and gathered on top of her head, and at the last minute, as she'd left the house, she had added her pearl necklace because a lady of 62 ought to leave the house looking proper. Years ago a nice lady she cleaned house for had given her those pearls. Missus Elder had said that she owned more jewels than she could ever wear and she had told Opal, then a young woman, that the pearls would be lovely with her cotton dresses.

"A girl named Opal should have some pearls. They'll light your face, just like that smile of yours," Missus Elder had said.

Opal pulled herself up the top step of the bus, holding tight to the chrome bar. Her vigor was not what it used to be all those years ago when she had picked cotton all day in the east Texas sun and watched the glistening young men working the fields with her, before Missus Elder had given her an indoor job. Aside from the bus driver, Opal saw only a young white man, scruffy and bearded, sitting in the first row of seats and a young woman near the back of the bus, her two young sons swarming around her like busy bees.

Opal smiled at the young mother as she walked to the back of the bus and took the seat behind the young family. The humidity of the day seeped through the open bus windows, holding her in place and loosening her hair from the tortoise shell hairpins. She pulled her embroidered hankie from her handbag and blotted her forehead. Opal had settled into her seat, her satchel tucked next to her, when she caught sight of bright, white eyes watching her beneath the bar at the top of the seat before her. Just as suddenly as she had seen the child's gaze, the boy's face vanished.

She was on her way to Tyler to visit her daughter and grandbabies. Opal's son, who lived with his family in the house next door to hers, had bought her the bus ticket. She had not seen her daughter for almost eighteen months, and there was now a new granddaughter, Ruby, born only two months ago. Ruby had two older brothers and Opal was eager to see her grandbabies again.

A movement pulled Opal from her thoughts and, again, the young boy in front of her caught her eye, his skin like a cup of coffee and his buzzed hair sparkling with the sunlight mingling with drops of sweat on his scalp. He was eyeing her; those probing wide eyes the color of mahogany and framed by lashes fit for a lass. The child's eyes latched onto her own gaze. Unflinching. He said nothing, but watched her intently as the bus bounced toward the north on the country road. His brother chattered away as he sat next to his mother, but the young boy in front of Opal stared at the old lady in the seat behind him. Opal would look away from the boy and watch out the window as the tall pine trees passed, broken every few miles by fields of cotton or beans, sights she found comforting. But it was August and the crops were turning brown, some already harvested. Her eyes always returned to find the sweet scamp watching her, his face gleeful and probing as if he were full of questions but afraid to ask.

The man up front got off at the next bus stop, but the young mother stayed. Over the next two hours, as the bus churned on toward

Tyler, stopping at a small town along the way where an elderly white couple boarded, the young boy continued to gaze at Opal and then would disappear behind the seat for a few moments. *Was it a game he played?*

Despite the scented talcum Opal had rubbed onto her skin before she dropped her satin slip over her shoulders that morning, she felt the bead of sweat gather at the nape of her neck and tickle her spine as it fell. It was indeed summertime, she thought. She had smiled at the young boy; only once did he return the smile, then disappeared again as if embarrassed he had revealed his teeth. Once she jolted awake after dozing off only to see the boy still peering. After all this reverence, Opal felt akin to him, but never was a word shared.

The bus rolled into Tyler and slowed to a stop at the bus station. Opal gathered her satchel and disembarked from the now empty bus. As her foot left the bottom step and found firm ground, the boy with the shining smile and mahogany eyes, a child who appeared to be about five or six years old, stood waiting for her.

He looked up at her. "I love my two grannies." He gazed again, as he had on the bus, and Opal smiled at him. "I love you too," he said. "One day I will marry you, and, to be certain, I am going to be a preacher."

"Oh, my," said Opal, surprised that he'd spoken, and when she blinked and looked again, he was gone. She never saw him again.

*   *   *

The young boy on the bus was now nothing but a memory, but a cherished one when it crossed her mind. It was the year when Opal turned 91 that she moved to the back room of her daughter's old home in Tyler. She could no longer walk without help and her son had brought her to stay with her granddaughter Ruby. Ruby and her husband lived in the home now, her parents having moved to Houston after selling the old house to their only daughter and her husband. Opal would stay with Ruby for the balance of her days.

"Ruby," she called.

"Yes, Granny?"

"Can you open the window? The mornin' sun is so pretty. And maybe there's a breeze," said Opal.

"Breakfast will be ready soon, Granny. I'll help you to the kitchen in a bit," said Ruby as the raised the window.

The sun often broke into shards of light as it passed through the tall pines, and Opal sometimes believed she was in her old church begging for the words of an old hymn. The long days could be lonely except on those rare days when Ruby's young nieces and nephews would visit from Houston and share a game of rummy.

Opal's memories filled her head, but even they came and went like the children who visited. She would hear the whispers between Ruby and her doctor. Recent memories faded and old ones surprised her at random. Her dementia worsened over time as the dreaded disease of lost words and recollections ravaged her daily joys, robbed her of the nostalgia she cherished. Yet there was that one memory of a small boy on a bus, a boy who professed his love and vanished ... that memory visited Opal often, most often coming with the morning sunlight. She did not know the boy's name, or had she forgotten it? She did not know if he became a preacher or even if he had been real. Her memories became nothing but a haze at times, but that day on the bus would come clear in her mind. *Did that sweet boy ever speak to his mom on that trip? I don't remember seeing the young mother speak to the playful boy, the one who had charmed her.* But she knew with all of her heart the child was a Godsend, a memory holding her close to her maker.

Etiquette vanished with her illness, and Opal spoke often, repeatedly, of fleeting moments, of picking blueberries with her mother as a child, the sunshine on the cotton fields, and of the boy on the bus. With her visions coming and going, Opal relayed her stories to anyone who would listen. The story of the boy on the bus was a vision she now recalled each day and openly shared, even to those who did not believe her story, to those who said she was only hallucinating.

In her sleep, in her dreams, the young boy would be there. Opal remembered his smile, his words, the few words she recalled. When she held those early visions, when they aimlessly appeared within her days that ran one to another without edges, she smiled. At times, especially in the darkness of night, fearsome visions of creatures and ghosts of friends now dead would visit, terrorizing her, startling her to cry out. Sometimes Ruby would come to comfort her.

"It's not real, Granny. See. There's nothing here," she would say.

"No. No. Look . . . over there. It's my grandpa. I see him there," Opal said, her voice still trembling.

"No one's there. Look. Nothing. Your grandpa is buried in Louisiana, long ago." Ruby switched on the nightlight.

"Let me get you some water, Granny," and Ruby would return with a glass and a pill. Opal resisted the medicine, but Ruby persisted until her grandmother swallowed it. Yet there were the days when Opal's visions were a fleeting recollection of her youth, like a visit from a friend. Through her journey to old age, even through the dark days when she could no longer find her own words, when faces near her seemed strange, the terrors receded and a hallowed calm surrounded her.

"She is near her end, Ruby," said Dr. Hudson. "Her breath is shallow, so you should prepare yourself."

"I miss her so much. She is not the lady I remember, except for her sweetness. Amidst her crazy visions, she always has her hope. We hate to let her go, yet some days she seems to rejoice in greeting that next journey," said Ruby. "Can you come by tomorrow?"

"Yes, Ruby, I will try to stop in tomorrow." He turned to leave, knowing there would likely be no need to come tomorrow.

That afternoon the house was quiet and Ruby's husband was at work. She tucked the cotton blanket tightly around her grandmother when Opal grasped Ruby's arm.

"That sweet boy. I see that sweet boy."

"Yes, grandma. You love that sweet boy."

"I do . . . and you," said Opal, pausing for a breath. She continued in a whisper. "The young boy . . . the one with the wide smile is now grown, right?" There was another measured breath.

"I know, Grandma. I know," said Ruby, consoling her grandmother.

"I love . . . you . . . Ruby," the words barely escaping her throat.

Ruby was startled at hearing her grandmother say her name, that Grandma remembered who she was. She kissed her grandmother's forehead.

"I love you too, Granny."

Walking out of the room to get a glass of water, she could not help but think how empty this house will be without Grandma Opal. As she returned with the water glass, she heard a firm knock at the front door. It was a cool fall day and she did not expect a visitor. She set the glass on the table by the bed and saw her grandmother's eyes were closed, her face serene.

"Grandma?" There was no response, and as Ruby reached for her grandmother's hand, she heard another knock beckon more urgently.

As she opened the front door, she saw a man she did not recognize. He was a tall handsome black man with compelling eyes the color of mahogany, not much older than herself. He smiled and a chill shuddered down Ruby's spine.

"Good day, ma'am. I'm Pastor Johnson. Opal is expecting me."

Why I Wrote This Story

The seeds of this short story were sparked from conversations I had, over time, with a beautiful woman in hospice, her visions of both the real and imagined and her memory of a sweet boy she'd met on a bus so many years ago. . . . Sandra Fox Murphy

THE ENIGMA CHRONICLES— REMEMBER THE FUTURE

Charles Breakfield & Rox Burkey

WOLFGANG'S CHESS GAME with Jacob had been great. With his win tonight, Jacob had played even better than his mother. Jacob had shared a few stories from when his Granny, Adriana, lived with him and his mother. Wolfgang tried not to dwell on things of the past, because it made him feel old and sad. When it was late, too quiet, and sleep wouldn't come, his mind would drift to the one thing in his life he wished he could have changed. It wasn't his fault. Nothing could have changed the outcome. But the nagging *what ifs* persisted. He reminded himself that his grandson Jacob was with him now. It had to be enough. Wolfgang was glad Jacob hadn't pushed for details.

In his mind, Wolfgang saw his vibrant, brilliant daughter Julianne laughing with his only love, Adriana. Both women were of medium height, lithe, and had wavy, flowing dark hair down their backs. Dresses were shorter than ever, stylish, and moved around them. A casual onlooker might think them sisters. They chattered and laughed while fixing special treats for their young male dinner guest. Even with the help employed in the chateau, Adriana took the time to tutor Julianne in cooking and other useful household skills. Everyone in the chateau was like family.

In the weeks leading up to that dinner, Julianne had only met with the young man in selected public settings. At no time were they unchaperoned. During those days in Europe, for the higher social echelon families, young women were not as restricted as before the war, but a lady's honor was still highly regarded. Her honor reflected not only on the family, but also on their business reputation. Julianne had recently admitted to her parents, after hours of conversation and walks in the public parks with Adriana nearby, that Andreas Müller was the man she wished as her partner. She wanted her parents to adore him as much as she did. Thus, the dinner.

For Julianne's extended family, there was a hope that each member would find a place in R-Group, the family business established at the tail end of WWII. Working toward that goal, Julianne was raised to extensively learn sciences, mathematics, history, literature, finances, new technologies, and languages, with the exclusion of the broader social interactions experienced by most European young people during the late 1960s. The dark cloud of the Soviet Iron Curtain hung over Europe, and it created a sense of urgency in all the family's activities. Their desire for preparedness in an uncertain future contributed to their choices.

To a large degree, Julianne had been sheltered during her education, except for two years attending a private, female-only university. Her loving parents protected her from certain things, while they expanded her knowledge far ahead of her peers in other ways. Social interactions were rare, so she was inexperienced in the large social venues of parties and dinners outside of the family. She was happily focused on study, travel, and work. Julianne was gifted with many talents, including languages, logic, and numbers. She was a happy, obedient child who never faltered in meeting her obligations as she grew up.

Andreas Müller had initially come into the family's bank, without the usual references used by most customers, to open accounts. When Julianne had turned 21, she'd taken on a role within the bank working with new customers; hence, she was called upon to help set up Andreas' accounts and verify his background. Wolfgang had also met with him briefly during this process. Andreas seemed charmed by Julianne and returned often to complete his transactions, always asking for Julianne. Though Andreas had been very attentive, and even formal, at his first meeting with Wolfgang, Wolfgang recalled something felt amiss. Nothing out of the ordinary was uncovered during the background checks, but Wolfgang remained guarded and unconvinced that Andreas was exactly who he seemed.

Wolfgang wanted to warn Julianne of his concerns, but he'd seen other parents within his social circle do this, and their children had resisted. Sadly, one had committed suicide and another had run away. Though he shared his concerns with Adriana, they agreed that to try to force anything on Julianne at her age was a mistake. They supported Julianne in her first experience with love, under layers of security and a watchful eye. During one late evening discussion, they laughed when they recalled the time when they were courting. Since they had been so much younger than Julianne was now, it hadn't been approved by Adriana's parents.

Dinner was a huge success, with great conversation among the four of them. Wolfgang admitted Andreas was quick-witted and made Julianne laugh. After dinner, Andreas challenged Wolfgang to a game of chess. Andreas played correctly but was no match for Wolfgang, and he good-naturedly admitted his defeat. The evening extended with coffee and stories of various family adventures. Toward the end of the evening, Andreas extended an invitation for Julianne to visit his parents' country home near Lake Zürich to celebrate the birthday of his best friend, Iwan. It was designed as a small, extended weekend holiday for the young pair, and two young ladies Julianne knew would be attending.

Adriana said she didn't know his parents and expressed concern about Julianne attending such an event. Andreas respectfully countered that few local families had met his parents, as his family had only recently moved to the estate on the lake. Julianne sensed that the request might be denied, so she suggested he let them discuss the details and confirm the following afternoon. He had good-naturedly accepted this as he bid his farewell after thanking them for the meal and great conversation. The evening had been exactly what one expected from a young man of means and good breeding.

The following morning was consumed with contacting friends regarding background on Andreas Müller and his family. His parents were quite private, and little information was discovered, outside of their passion for travel. The estate was paid for in cash, and a full staff was employed to maintain the high standards of that region. It was said by others living near the lake that his parents often traveled but had been pleasant in their social interactions. How the senior Müller earned his income was unclear yet positively speculated. The family had money, but privacy for the Swiss was never questioned.

Adriana finally confirmed that the two young ladies, daughters of friends, would be in attendance. After speaking with Wolfgang, they agreed Julianne could attend and take Crissy, one of the housemaids, with her to help with gowns and hair. It would be a long weekend with several activities planned including sailing, horseback riding, walks on the lake, and meals. Julianne was ecstatic and blushed as she called Andreas to convey her acceptance. He planned to collect her and the two other young ladies the following Friday morning in his car. He reassured Adriana and Wolfgang that he would watch out for Julianne and promised she would phone when they arrived.

When Julianne returned from the weekend, she was bubbling with excitement over all the things she'd seen and done. She enjoyed his two friends, Iwan and Bartek. Lily, one of the young ladies, thought the young men were wonderfully educated and brilliant. Julianne was more in love than ever and asked for Andreas to be included in more family dinners. During the times he visited over the next few weeks, they walked in the lavish chateau gardens, enjoyed lively conversation, delicious meals, and games of chess. Wolfgang wasn't totally won over, like Adriana, but he was warming to the young man. Andreas seemed to have a head for business, though it was unclear what his exact business ventures were. He had said quite seriously at one point that they were extremely top secret.

One moonlit evening, as Julianne and Andreas strolled the garden, they paused at one of the benches to enjoy the scents and muted sounds of the garden. Andreas took her hand and moved to bended knee, then declared his love for her as he slipped a brilliant marques diamond set in white gold onto her finger. It fit perfectly. Both surprised and delighted, Julianne had thrown her arms around him and said, "Oh, yes. I would love to be your wife."

The happy couple returned to the library to share the news. Wolfgang winced as he recalled his lingering reservations regarding Andreas, but the happiness in the eyes of his daughter won him over. She was over 21 and could do as she wished. He graciously gave them his blessing, and they all drank a toast.

Many weeks later as plans for the wedding proceeded, Wolfgang realized they had grown less cautious in keeping a watchful eye. Julianne was away more in the evenings with Andreas alone, or with his friends at dinners out or dancing. Julianne gushed over these events, but for Julianne it was all thrilling and fun, feelings that upon reflection she was ill-prepared to handle.

Two weeks before the wedding date, Julianne began to miss meals and retreated to her bedroom suite with headaches and other maladies. Adriana was concerned, but thought it was because of the work and wedding planning that was taking away from their normal rest. Even she was tired and worn out at the end of each day. Adriana insisted that Julianne needed her rest, as the planned six-month honeymoon would be very tiresome, especially with the first stop in Africa. Wolfgang was worried but acquiesced to the wise counsel of his wife.

One week before the wedding, Wolfgang received a request from his friend François, in Paris, to come and visit. They did business together often, with Wolfgang advising him on investments. François worked at Interpol, and he and his wife were old family friends. Wolfgang agreed to take the train the next day to meet for a late lunch and catch up, as well as discuss business. Wolfgang planned to stay the night and return to Zürich the following day.

The train ride was uneventful, and their lunch meeting was at a charming bistro where François filled Wolfgang in on all his family's changes. As Wolfgang's oldest customer, the conversation was all about François first and foremost. It was just the sort of distraction Wolfgang needed after weeks of wedding plans. He'd recently discovered that the father of the bride's main role revolved around the funding aspects. After lunch they went to François' office to go over some additional business items and sign papers. Wolfgang presented the investment summaries with all the current numbers and projections. His recommendations for investment shifts included new technology shifts the R-Group had deemed beneficial for their customers.

With business concluded, François shifted in his chair and made the fateful declaration that rocked Wolfgang's world. "Wolfgang, do you recall you asked me to check on the background of young Andreas Müller? It took far longer than you would have wished, but I have found some troubling information."

Wolfgang recalled the way his chest clinched, and the excellent food he'd just consumed seemed to sour in his stomach. Time was suspended. He unsuccessfully tried to school his features, while his insides broke into tiny pieces. The only thought to cross his mind was that at least it was before the wedding.

François looked at the change in his friend with concern, then continued, "I sense this information worries you. Let me give you the facts.

"Andreas Müller is one of several aliases used by a young man who meets the description you sent to me. It has taken extensive man hours to look through various documents, but this young man has a history of targeting young women and charming them while he gains information on their families. Blackmail seems to be his focus, though he has ties which suggest espionage. He has been deemed a deep spy by both Scotland Yard and Interpol, is on the payroll of the KGB, and if found will be arrested on sight. He's known to sell his information to the highest bidder.

"Additionally, he has left a trail of broken-hearted ladies over the last 10 or so years, under as many names. He is not to be trusted, especially with any of your business or family information. Anything you can do to help us apprehend this spy would be appreciated."

Ever one to keep his thoughts close to his chest, Wolfgang calmly replied, "You are certain? Do you have any photographs of this man, just to verify? I have had him to dinner a few times, but I didn't feel him as a threat to my business."

"Yes, I do have a couple of photographs. With more and more people getting the Polaroid cameras, we are actually expanding our files with more casual photos. I think it will help with our crime fighting in the future, don't you?"

Wolfgang nodded agreement, as he looked at the photos of Andreas with one smiling young lady after another at his side. Wolfgang saw that life as his family knew it had just changed forever. Wolfgang doubted that Andreas had any idea how people were documenting information these days. After thanking François for the information and the meal, then promising to alter the investments as they had discussed, he excused himself and caught the last train home.

When he arrived at the chateau, he was surprised to find Adriana awake and waiting for him. Before he could relate what he'd discovered, Adriana fell into his arms and announced that Julianne was with child and was beside herself, feeling she'd let her family down. When Adriana had tried to reassure her that the wedding would take place and everything would work out, Julianne had cried even harder.

Julianne finally explained that she'd told Andreas she suspected she was pregnant, and he'd laughed at her foolishness. Andreas had told her they were never going to marry and that the ring he had gifted her was plaster. Adriana had pressed her for more information and discovered he had also demanded some confidential bank information, which to this point Julianne had refused to provide. Julianne may have been foolish about him, but never about the family business. After confronting him with his responsibility, he threatened her with scandal by personally spreading her news on the society pages, unless she provided the information in three days.

Wolfgang was furious, mostly with himself for not voicing his early concerns. Even in these modern times, such a scarlet branding would be impossible to overcome. The loyalty Julianne had for her family was at her very core. He paced the room for several minutes trying to determine the best course of action. Then he explained what François had related regarding Andreas' background. Wolfgang was confident that the rogue had met his match, as a plan of sorts started to take shape.

Julianne was brought into their room with red-rimmed eyes and resignation evident in her stance. Recalling this and the hours of discussion that followed still caused Wolfgang real pain as he had watched their lives unravel. He held his girls and tried to be strong.

She stoically explained she was in charge of her own fate. Julianne understood the importance of the family business and knew their friends would shun them, all because of her foolishness. Marriage to anyone in their society would elude her. Julianne's only request was that her baby never be told.

Julianne had wanted to leave the country before Andreas could ruin her and the family. Wolfgang said they might discuss that but outlined what he considered the first step, which was to get Andreas behind bars. Wolfgang explained the details of what François had related and how he felt the authorities could be discreet.

Over the next two days they finalized their plan. Wolfgang was correct in that the authorities promised discretion as they set up to capture the spy at the bank. Julianne called Andreas for a meeting at the bank, which Andreas, knowing he was getting a payoff, agreed to meet at noon. He no sooner arrived and asked for Julianne, when the authorities apprehended him. As Andreas was escorted out, he said vile things about his victim, who he termed, *Julianne the Fornicatress*. Fortunately, the bank had been cleared of customers, and the employees who heard the ravings of the rogue had deep loyalties to the family. Julianne held her head high as she left the bank, knowing in her heart she would never work there again. She needed to make a future for herself and her child where no one knew her.

By the evening meal her tears were dried. Julianne outlined her now finalized plans to leave Zürich and go to the United States. She explained that when Andreas first rejected her, she had contacted two of her friends from school who had moved to New York to work for Bell Labs. Julianne had asked about potential openings, as she had been learning programming while working for the bank. They had called back and assured her of a position on the team. They even offered her a place to stay for a while.

Wolfgang was brokenhearted. Adriana was visibly stricken at the idea of her daughter going to a foreign country on her own. An argument ensued, and Adriana insisted she go with her daughter, as she was also an accomplished bank programmer who could help Julianne get established. She planned to return after Julianne was settled. It was this decision that haunted Wolfgang. He wanted to go along, but Adriana insisted he needed to mind the business and keep it going for Julianne and her child. Several days later they said goodbye for the first of many times to follow over the years.

Now Wolfgang agonized over what, if anything, to tell Jacob. The same day Julianne and Adriana left, Andreas had eliminated Wolfgang's chance at revenge by taking a cyanide capsule while in custody. In the end, Andreas wasn't man enough to undergo a rigorous interrogation or own his mistakes.

Wolfgang knew one cannot share the ugly secrets for the harm they always do. Secrets like this make you feel old. He knew he was old. As he sat with his head in his hands, he wished sleep would come so he could dream back his life.

Why I Wrote This Story

The Enigma Chronicles Introduction. Our Enigma Book Series is within the techno thriller genre because of how three young men captured a copy of the Enigma machine during World War II. They and their families escaped to Switzerland, days ahead of the German invasion. This background is not detailed in any of the novels and is focused on the founding members of the R-Group. We have used The Enigma Chronicles term within some of the chapter headings of our award winning series to identify key elements of a story impacted by *the three pillars of the R-Group. The Enigma encryption machine and the effort to break the code ushered in the computer age. These men who formed the R-Group could not have foreseen how their moral fiber would set the benchmark in battling cyber evil in the 21st century. We believe that ethics and moral code have the best chance of properly navigating the cyber criminals of today. The Enigma Chronicles are designed as shorts to tell the back stories of history that shed light on the present. This is the first, and we welcome your feedback. Thank you,* **Breakfield** *and* **Burkey**

TWENTY-TEN

Joe Kilgore

WHIT OPENED HIS eyes and slowly the clock on his bedside table came into focus. The time was twenty minutes before ten. Ordinarily this would have meant nothing to him. But today was December 31, 2009. Which meant that his last wake-up before the year twenty-ten occurred at exactly twenty minutes to ten. Strange coincidence, he thought. Then he thought, fuck coincidence, I have to pee.

Splashing water on his face and trying to decide whether or not to shave, the numbers found their way into his thoughts again. I was twenty years old when I came out here. I gave myself ten years to make it and I sure as shit didn't. Now I'll be going home January 1, 2010. Pretty funny, huh? But he didn't feel like laughing, or shaving. So he just grabbed a shower.

After dressing and running a comb through his hair, he pocketed his wallet with the built-in money clip, painfully aware there were only two bills there. When he looked to see what they were, he shook his head. He was holding a twenty and a ten.

Outside, the sun's glare smacked him like a 10K bounced off a reflector. Whit slipped on his shades and walked the twenty or so yards up the block to the Daily Grind. It was the last place left in the neighborhood where he hadn't boosted a tip or walked a check.

He ordered coffee black while he sat under an awning and wondered where the hell the last decade had gone.

Nobody starts out to be a cliché. Whit certainly didn't. He was convinced he was going to make it in show business. Sure, he was just another wide-eyed kid from the Midwest, but he was good looking, willing to work hard and ready to pay his dues. Plus, he did have something special. What was it his drama coach called it? Oh yeah, vulnerability. That was it . That vulnerable quality like a Montgomery Clift or a James Dean or a Jake Gyllenhaall in Brokeback Mountain. Okay, so his drama teacher was gay. Whose wasn't?

But Whit just knew he'd make it. Well, he knew it for a while. He knew it until the auditions went nowhere and agents lost interest and modeling jobs dried up. Then he kidded himself while he waited tables and fantasized about being discovered. When he realized he wasn't going to be plucked out of oblivion by a producer, director, or fading star, he knew he was just killing time. That's when he started spending off-hours with various hangers-on who always had a story about how close they were to some big wig, high roller or rapper cum gangster. From there it didn't take long to find himself hanging with druggies, miscreants, petty criminals and soon-to-be felons. Little wonder Whit then occasionally lifted a purse from the chair of an inattentive diner. Or bounced off a fender and convinced the driver that for a couple of hundred there was no need to call the cops, insurance company or the attorney that Whit didn't really have. And by the time he was elbowing glass panes out of back doors where everybody had Play Stations but nobody had security systems, he had long since lost the dream of turning his vulnerability into fame and fortune.

But through all that, Whit never forgot the promise he made himself. The deal to give Hollywood a ten-year shot and if he hadn't made good, to just walk away. Well, the ten years were up. And he had no problem accepting that all he had succeeded at was failure. Nothing's going to change that in one day, Whit told himself as he sipped his coffee and looked at the clock in the shop window across the street. The clock that read twenty minutes past ten.

Before he could obsess over the continuing confluence of twenties and tens, a black Escalade rolled between him and the shop window. It parked square in his eye line. The windows were tinted. He couldn't see inside. For almost a minute nothing happened. Then the front passenger door opened and out stepped Silky.

Silky was the polar opposite of his nickname. Emaciated, jittery, constantly disheveled, stubble-faced, slack-jawed and perennially dyspeptic, he was the poster boy for what nobody wanted to become. But if you hung out for any length of time near La Cienega and Santa Monica Boulevard, you were apt to make his acquaintance.

"Whit, is that you behind them Foster Grants?"

"They're Serengetis. But yeah, it's me."

"How you afford that?"

"Stiffed the landlord. After today, it won't matter."

"Still gonna' leave town, huh?"

"Got my bus ticket already. Here in my pocket."

"Let me see."

Whit reached into his pocket, pulled out the ticket and handed it to Silky.

With a cigarette dangling from his cracked lips, he read aloud, "L A to Chicago. Bus twenty ten. Leaves—"

"You're kidding," Whit cut in, "that's not really the bus number, is it?"

"A number's a number," Silky slurred. "Who gives a flying fuck."

"It's just weird," Whit started, "I've been seeing this number all over and—"

"Listen, forget the number," Silky mumbled as he sat down, leaned in close and fogged Whit's coffee with whisky breath. "I got a way for you to get out of town in style"

"Oh yeah, Whit answered. "Who do I have to kill?"

"Glad you asked, amigo." Then looking around to see if anyone was listening,

Silky added, "Take a look at this."

He opened his jacket just wide enough for Whit to see a stack of Benjamins in his pocket.

"Where did you get that?"

"From my, and what could be your, benefactor. One quick job tonight and you leave town tomorrow a rich man."

"Yeah. How rich?"

"Twenty grand, friend. Ten now, the rest after."

"Jeeze," Whit said, his head rolling back in disbelief. "Somebody is trying to tell me something."

"Right," Silky grinned. "Somebody like me."

Whit continued to quiz him. "What do you get out of this?"

"The same," Silky replied. For a finder's fee, driving the car and keeping my big mouth shut. I've already got my up-front. Contingent of course, on delivering a trigger man."

"Trigger man? You're really talking about a hit? I've never done anything like that."

"There's a first time for everything. And you're the perfect choice, man. It's done tonight. You're out of town tomorrow. Nobody's the wiser. Plus, you go home a big man. Not just another loser."

God, Whit thought. Maybe something incredible is happening. All those twenty-ten numbers. Now this. I never thought of myself as a killer. Sure, I've crossed the line enough times to warrant hard time. But this is the big one. When will *I* ever have a chance to pocket twenty thousand dollars again? Something's screwy here though. He's not telling me all of it.

"Silky, why don't *you* just do this thing and pocket all the cash?

"You got what I don't have, Whit. You got style. I'd be spotted for a plant in a minute. But you got looks, personality, and you don't look like a tough guy. Nobody would take you for a killer. You look like you'd be the one who'd be . . . what's the word"

"Vulnerable?"

"Yeah, you got that vulnerable thing going."

"Hasn't done much for me," Whit said.

"It's about to pay off big," Silky replied.

Whit looked back at the imposing sport utility vehicle. "Money-man in there?"

"Nearest thing. It's the guy who works for the guy footin' the bill.

All you got to do is step in, let him look you over, and answer a couple of questions. It's a go or no-go on the spot."

"I guess it can't hurt to listen," Whit said.

"Swell, but don't ask him his or his boss's name. He won't ask yours. Less we all know about each other the better."

The driver looked wide as the Escalade's wheelbase. He didn't turn when Whit got in the backseat. He just stared into the rear-view mirror and spoke in a guttural growl.

"Take the shades off. Want to see your eyes."

A cheeky request, Whit thought, since the guy was wearing mirrored aviators. But he did what he was told.

"Pretty boy, huh? Yeah. His looks will do."

Whit wasn't sure it was a compliment. He didn't respond. The man spoke again.

"How about guts, pretty boy. Got the balls to do this thing?"

For some unknown reason, Whit reacted like he was at an impromptu audition. In the most insolent tone he could muster, he spat back, "You want to see them too, Mary?"

Silky's smoke fell into his lap. But he just sat frozen, waiting for the big man's response. After a short silence that felt long to both Whit and Silky, the big man giggled. "Damn. You said the guy was an actor, Silky. You were right, he's like that fuckin' Marvin Brando." Silky chuckled along with him. Whit sat there trying to figure out why he had been crazy enough to pop off.

Then the big guy laid it out for Whit in his own vernacular. The target was a Hollywood asshole named Randy Weaver. A douche bag who was into the behemoth's boss for nearly seven figures. His boss felt the dummy didn't have the dough to pay him so it made more business sense to whack the dude and show those movie high-rollers that the last thing anyone wanted to do was stiff the goose laying the powdered white eggs. Once they saw what happened to people who welched, they'd shit their lace panties and his boss would never have another problem in cinema city. The chunky boy had a way with words.

"But what's the actual plan?" Whit asked.

This time Silky answered. He told Whit that there was a party that night at Weaver's house. Whit would attend the party. At twenty minutes to midnight, Weaver would go out to the pool ahead of the guests who would be getting their New Year's party regalia in the music room. Weaver would come out early to accept the latest delivery. Whit was the delivery boy. Except the delivery would be one to the chest, then two to the head. Silky added that the pool was on a hillside and all Whit had to do was go over the retaining wall, and down the hill. Silky would be waiting on the street below in the getaway car.

"You don't have a car," Whit said.

Silky flashed his jacket open again revealing the cash, "I will have shortly."

"But I don't have a gun," Whit countered, trying to add some reality to the lunacy that seemed to be floating around him.

"You'll use this one," the boulder behind the wheel said as he pulled a stubby black pistol out of his breast pocket and handed it to Whit. "It's a Llama Minimax Subcompact. Don't fuck around with it before you need it tonight. It's loaded."

Whit started to say, "I'm not that familiar with this brand of—"

The big guy cut him off. "See that safety on the side."

Whit pointed to what he hoped was the safety.

"Yeah. Just flip that down, point and pull the trigger. But don't try to be no Andy Oakley," he added. "Get close enough so you can't miss."

"But all the other guests will hear the shots," Whit protested."

Once again, the lummox reached in his pocket. This time extracting a five-inch metal cylinder. "Nobody won't hear nothin' cause you'll screw this on the end of your piece. Presto. You got a silencer. You're James fuckin' Bond.

Whit continued to look for loopholes. "But they don't know me. Why should they let me in."

King Kong reached down, opened the compartment between the bucket seats and pulled out a brown envelope. "You got an engraved invitation. It's in here along with ten g's. Half your payment. You and Silky get your other half when it's done."

Whit felt the weight of the money in the envelope. He'd never held that much cash in his life. He couldn't believe that in a few hours it would be twice as heavy.

"Okay," big boy said, "you took the money and the gun. It's a go." Then his fat head swiveled around wrinkling his neck like a towel being wrung, and he looked right into Whit's eyes. "And don't get no ideas about usin' that ten grand to split. We'll find you. Then we'll hurt you so bad you'll beg us to kill you. Then we will." He turned around, started the engine and said, "Now both of you get the fuck out."

Later, in his apartment, Whit sat looking at the cash he had spread out on his bed. He had counted it over and over. In the middle of it was the gun with the silencer screwed onto the barrel. He had practiced attaching it over and over. On top of the gun was the invitation, which had been flipped on its face because Silky had written on the back of it the time he'd be by to pick Whit up. Twenty-minutes to ten.

In the convertible that Silky had rented from Budget, Whit looked straight ahead and tried to come to grips with how things had come so far so fast. But those thoughts kept getting jumbled up with competing ones about whether or not he could really go through with it. And all the while Silky was feeding him more information.

"See that hill. The pools on top of it. You just shimmy down that sucker and I'll be waiting here."

"Are you sure you'll be here?"

"I'll be here. Just remember . . . at the pool twenty of midnight. You got ten minutes before the guests come out. Just pop the asshole and get down the hill. Then we ride off into the New Year richer than we already are."

Whit wanted to ask Silky if he could really trust the big guy to give them the rest of their dough, but they were pulling into the circular drive and his thoughts immediately sprang back to the task at hand. He got out of the car and Silky drove away quickly.

The house reminded Whit of old films he had seen. It was a two-story stucco with a green tile roof, wooden shutters, leaded windows and ornate hardware on the dark front door. For a moment he just stood there, silently asking himself if he could really go through with this. Then Whit patted himself just to make sure everything was in place. Gun in one breast pocket. Silencer in the other. Invitation in one outer pocket. Bus ticket in the other. Cash stuffed in all his other pockets and the soles of his shoes. He couldn't bring himself to part with it.

Whit rang the doorbell. A butler answered, took the invitation and showed him in. Whit could hear music and voices coming from a room on his right. He turned to walk in that direction, but all of a sudden, his legs felt like bridge pilings. He couldn't move them. Take it easy, he told himself. It's just stage fright. And why not? This was easily the biggest role of his career.

Before he knew it, he had somehow made it to the bar. No one had spoken to him on the way. He ordered a Scotch and had taken a couple of man-sized gulps before fear struck him again. Jesus, he hadn't even asked what Weaver looked like. How could he be sure the right person would be by the pool. Again, he told himself not to freeze up. He could find out. But he'd have to initiate contact to do it. Whit looked around the room and selected what he thought was a good candidate for conversation. A young woman in a soft, flowered dress. She had short hair and dark eyes and a smile that seemed to say it's all going to be okay. He walked over to her and said, "Hi, my name's Whit. I was wondering if you'd seen Randy?"

"Randi who," she said with a question mark in her eyes.

"Randy Weaver."

"Well silly, I'm Randi Weaver."

Whit's jaw dropped to his shirt collar.

"Close your mouth," she said, "flies will get in."

"You're Ran . . . you're Weaver. You own this house?"

Then a spark of recognition came over her. "Oh, you must be from—." But she stopped her sentence before she finished it. And her smile quickly turned sour while her tone turned caustic. "Listen, didn't they tell you how this was going to work. The pool at twenty before midnight. You'll give me the stuff there. I don't want to see or talk to you until then. So just stand around and drink. Or mingle if you know how. But leave me alone until then."

Whit started to say he understood but he couldn't get a word out before she spun and walked away. A woman, thought Whit. A young woman at that. Okay, kind of a bitch, but still a woman. Can I kill a woman? Better sit down and think this out, he reasoned. He found a leather lounger and just sat there thinking and drinking. In fact, the only time he got up in the next hour and a half was to go to the bar. Which he did twice. But it didn't help. He still wasn't sure what he was going to do.

At 11:30 the crowd started making their way to the music room. Whit fell in at the back of the pack drifting off when the gaggle passed the entrance to the pool. He no longer had his drink in his hand. His hands were thrust in his pants' pockets where the cash kept reminding him why he was there. He walked to the far side of the pool and looked at the ledge. It wouldn't take much to hoist himself over and head down the hill. The angle however, kept him from seeing whether Silky was waiting below.

As he stood there, his hands seemed to move involuntarily to his breast pockets. First the gun. Then the silencer. Then he was attaching one to the other just as he had practiced in his room. Then he tried to blot out all thought except for scenes he had seen countless times in movies where the cold-blooded killer simply raises his arm and fires. He lost track of time thinking. Until he heard her voice.

"Okay lets have it."

She was walking toward him. He turned and walked toward her, the gun down by his side. When she was a few feet from him, she said, "We haven't got all night."

Whit raised the weapon and pointed it at her.

"Christ," she said, "what are you doing?"

Whit had no answer. He just stood there with his arm extended, the barrel aimed at her chest.

"Oh God, no! Please don't. Please don't," she whimpered.

Whit's hand began to shake and his arm felt like an anchor was dragging it down.

"Don't kill me. Please don't kill me!" She cried.

For a split second, Whit couldn't move at all. Then the ache in his arm became unbearable and he let it drop by his side. "I'm sorry, I don't really know why I came," he said. His mind seemed strangely blank. He couldn't seem to focus. He was here, standing before this trembling woman. All he had to do was raise his arm once again and fire. But he could summon neither the will nor the strength to do either. Then his tenuous grip loosened even more. The pistol slipped from his hand and clattered on the concrete. Whit managed a hapless, rather vulnerable smile, turned and walked away.

As he was beginning to hoist himself over the retaining wall, almost simultaneously he heard a muffled *pop* and a *thud*, as a piece of the wall shattered near his hand. Then he looked around and saw her coming toward him. Tears had run the mascara down her cheeks, but her eyes were wide with fury. She held the pistol in front of her with both hands as she screamed, "Try to kill me, will you . . . I'll get you, you fuck!"

Pop. Thud. Another piece of the wall chunked loose beside him. Adrenalin kicked in and Whit leapt over the wall and started scrambling down the hill like a startled gecko. Limbs were flashing by, leaves slid underfoot, a boulder in the shadows caught him square in one knee and he went down hard. He started to rub it when a spray of dirt and leaves exploded by his side. Jesus, she's coming down after me, he realized. He didn't even take time to get up, he just propelled himself down the hill using his butt for a sled while bumping over broken limbs and rocks as he descended.

Whit hit the ditch at the bottom of the hill and would have rolled into the street had it not been for the convertible parked there. Silky, having heard Whit's noisy descent, had thrown the car in park and scrambled over the bucket seats to see what had landed.

Gasping for breath, Whit looked up at Silky and said, "I couldn't do it. She's coming after me."

"She?" Silky said incredulously. Quickly followed by, "Mother-fuck! Don't you know what they'll do to us? I'll get the bitch." He pulled a huge revolver from his waist band, jumped from the car and started up the incline.

Whit tried to protest but Silky didn't wait to listen. He disappeared into the darkness while Whit started brushing himself off. Seconds later Whit heard three rapid, muffled pops, immediately followed by a resounding crack. For an instant, there was silence. Then the rustle of leaves and the breaking of twigs and the tumbling of rocks told Whit something was coming down the hill fast. Before he had time to move, Silky slammed into the ditch. But that didn't stop the noise. Whit had to jump to his right quickly to avoid Randi's somersaulting arms and legs as she too barreled against the side of the car.

It didn't take a genius to see they'd shot each other. The left half of Randi's chest was shredded. Blood and dirt were all over what was left of her dress. Silky was no better. He had holes in his throat, jaw and ear. The back of his head looked like a ripe water melon. Whit checked to see if either was breathing. Neither was. He realized there was nothing more he could do for them. But, it came to him, maybe there was something he could do for himself. That's when he opened Silky's coat. The cash was still there. He transferred it to his own jacket, walked around the car and got in on the driver's side.

Somehow, Whit's shock, which had paralyzed him moments before, had vanished. All of a sudden everything was blindingly clear. The job was done and the bad guys actually saved money. Silky was the only one who knew his name and he wouldn't be saying anything to anyone. In a few hours, he'd be gone with more than enough to start a brand new life. A smile came over Whit's face. Perhaps his drama teacher had been dead wrong. Maybe he wasn't vulnerable after all. Maybe he was just flat out lucky.

Whit took one last look at the lights of L A. Then he fastened his seat belt, threw the car in gear and burned rubber as the dashboard clock rolled over to twelve a.m. It was New Year's Day, Twenty-Ten.

Why I Wrote This Story

I wanted to write the kind of story you used to see in the old film noirs of the 1940's and early 1950's. But I wanted to make it contemporary enough so that it still had relevance to today's audiences. In classic noir, the hero is more or less doomed from the beginning. I wondered if perhaps there was a way to juggle the structure a bit and wind up with something that fit the genre but still provided a bit of a twist at the end. Readers will have to determine whether or not I was successful at doing that.

FAITHFUL FOREVER

Robert DeLuca

M Y WIFE TOLD me up front that I was absolutely foolish to do it. I knew she was right (she usually is), but as usual I was too pigheaded to listen. After all I was retired, had time on my hands, and spent a career in real estate. It only made sense when I was asked to take over our local subdivision homeowners association that I do it. I was surely qualified and felt I could change a few things to the benefit of everyone. Oh, boy was I wrong.

The HOA had been run by the same group of "good old" folks for many years. As long as the grass got cut and the home assessments didn't go up, no one much cared what went on at the HOA meetings. I had served on the Board of Directors for a year. During that time while I never observed an outright wrong doing, it did bother me that there was little regard for accounting controls or following the deed restrictions and by-laws as they were written. Board meetings were basically parties where we enjoyed beer, wine, snacks, and only occasionally discussed neighborhood matters. Actually, that approach may not be quite as bad as it seems since there wasn't much real business to conduct anyway.

Under my administration I intended to at least "right the ship" by running things in accordance to the rules in place. I spent lots of time redrafting the by-laws and setting up simple accounting guidelines. My simple goal was to do things correctly by the book. I had no interest in making major changes. Wouldn't it have been nice to balance the checkbook every so often? Apparently not, the carry over good old boys (And, yes, I do mean "old") board members had zero interest in changing anything. "We've always done it that way." "Oh, you can trust her." "That bank makes so many mistakes." "No one on the board will vote for that." "You are not at all like Fred, our former president." "No, we don't need a reserve account." And on and on. It was so bad that if *I* was for "it", *they* were against "it", no matter what "it" was. Why hadn't I listened to my wife?

After only the first few meetings my frustration already morphed to grudging acceptance, and I began to count the number of months until my term would be over. Then one day, quite surprisingly, one of the old guard abruptly resigned from the board. I guess she was sick of dealing with me. All of a sudden there was a vacancy to be filled. Had I been a more astute politician at the outset I would have stacked the board with my team, but live and learn. At least now I could appoint a replacement, who might at least hear me out before saying "no." A name immediately came to mind.

Our next door neighbor was an elderly gentleman, who at one time was a senior engineer in the Gemini space program at NASA in Clear Lake City. We had gotten to know both Jimmy Anthony and his wife, Annie, fairly well. They were a wonderful and warm couple, whom we admired. Jimmy was tall, and still had a shock of grey hair that lent him almost a distinguished professor look. He was soft spoken, and always considered what he was about to say before he opened his mouth. He was amiable, highly intelligent, and blessed with a self-depreciating sense of humor. It was impossible not to like Jimmy. Annie was his perfect compliment. She was a perky blonde and barley over five feet. Always bright and cheery, she prattled on incessantly. Annie never met a stranger and was a gracious hostess. In days gone by, the Anthony house on a corner lot was the neighborhood way station for gossip and kicking back. Everyone was welcome on their back patio to share a cocktail or two and unwind for the day.

It was a foreboding afternoon a few years back. Jimmy sat across the kitchen table and stared lovingly at his darling wife, who had just hung up the phone. The news was not good. A long history of cigarettes had caught up to his precious Annie. In the months that followed she fought a valiant fight as she wasted away but finally left a heart broken Jimmy to join the Lord about a year before I took over the HOA. Jimmy was devastated by the loss. He wasn't prepared to cope without someone who had been his whole life. Never forthcoming in his own right, with all his joy gone, he withdrew totally into a shell. Though they had been frequent church goers, Jimmy rarely went without Annie. We made it a point to drop in on him from time to time. He was always cordial but was clearly still struggling to come to grips with his grief. Occasionally, we'd see him out in his yard, but for the most part he remained cloistered inside with the TV on or reading a book.

Jimmy had to be my guy to fill the board vacancy. I knew he was intelligent and got along well with others. More importantly, if I could convince him to join the board, maybe, just maybe, it would get him out of his funk. At first he wasn't interested, but after more than a little badgering I was at least able to get him to a meeting to see what went on.

When I stopped by to pick him up I half expected that he'd turn me away, but he was ready to go. In fact, once we were sitting around the table, I discovered that Jimmy already knew almost everyone there. My agenda, which was crammed with critical business items (ha ha), went largely ignored that evening as Jimmy Anthony renewed old acquaintances. He really seemed to be enjoying himself, which pleased me very much. Indeed, before the end of that meeting Jimmy was unanimously voted in as a new director. I was ecstatic. It had taken me several months, but I finally got something approved!

One of our board members in particular, Catherine White seemed especially pleased to see Jimmy. Many years ago, Catherine's husband, John, had worked with Jimmy at NASA, and the couples had been close friends. Unfortunately, after John passed away of a heart attack some ten years earlier, Jimmy and Annie lost contact with Catherine even though she lived alone only a few blocks away. Unlike Jimmy, though, Catherine was able to adjust and deal with her loss. She made it a point to stay active, joined clubs (including our infamous hard working board), and attended neighborhood social activities. She was approaching eighty and the years had left her a bit stooped, but she had her hair done regularly and still always dressed well. Catherine White was perhaps best known for the devilish twinkle that still sparked in her bright blue eyes.

At the next board meeting, which was Jimmy's first as an official director, it was hard to tell how things were going with him. He offered little but seemed to follow the discussion, which was consistent with his taciturn nature. As soon as I thought I could get away with it I glanced at my watch and was debating whether I could end the fascinating session a little early, when a curious thing happened. With a furtive glance in Jimmy's direction, Catherine suddenly blurted out "You know I am very upset about all the pick-up trucks sitting in our streets at all hours of the day and night. We need to do something."

Now this is Texas and besides Longhorns, the pickup is by far the most sacred animal we have. The outburst from Catharine was not in keeping with her usual affable go-with-the- flow demeanor. I suspected something was up. None of the other directors, had any reaction to her outlandish statement. They never did unless it was my suggestion.

Then even more bizarrely, Jimmy of all people piped up in a bold assertive voice that I didn't know he had, "Catherine, you know that is outright nonsense. Pickup trucks are more common than cars. I am amazed that you would suggest such a ridiculous thing."

If Catherine was upset, she did not let on. She snapped right back. "Well, you know, Jimmy, if you got out more maybe you'd see exactly what I am talking about." I saw the twinkle; she had awoken the slumbering bear.

Summoning what little authority I could muster, I tabled that "hot button" discussion until next time and adjourned the meeting. On the way home, Jimmy never stopped talking about the encounter and how that "poor old thing was" out of touch. If nothing else, I was heartened to see some life left in the old boy. I was a little concerned that the pickup truck clash might give rise to a rift between Jimmy and Catherine, but I need not have worried. Despite the initial confrontation their interaction from then on was hardly hostile. In fact, it seemed quite the opposite. During the next few meetings a rapport arose between the two old friends, who now managed to next to each other. Had Jimmy's shell cracked a bit? I wasn't certain, but he sure talked a lot more, and we even saw him at church on Sunday.

It is my practice to let our large bullmastiff walk me each evening on a route that passes right by Jimmy's front door. The heat of the day had eased as the monster dog began to pull me along. As we approached Jimmy's house I saw a white Ford LTD pull up in front of the mailbox. I thought the driver looked familiar, and as we drew even with the car I recognized Catherine sitting there. She didn't get out but rolled down the window to say hello. While standing there chatting I noticed a covered glass casserole dish of some sort on the seat next to her. She didn't mention it, and I didn't ask. Well wasn't that interesting?

Over the next several weeks, it was the unspoken talk of the neighborhood. You had to be blind not to notice Jimmy's car in her driveway and vice versa. My pup and I saw them every so often strolling together on the walking path that winds through our neighborhood. The tall distinguished man craning his neck so as not to miss one word from the animated stooped little lady as they eased slowly along. There was no denying that a mutual fondness had arisen between them. It was very obvious in our meetings. Nobody mentioned it, but nobody missed it either. The transformation in Jimmy Anthony was remarkable. I couldn't be around him when we didn't discuss the Astros' prospects, politics, or even the weather. In the months after he lost Annie he had become almost distant. Now that his life had taken on more meaning, he was a changed man. At times he was almost jolly. I was thrilled for both of them. A Las Vegas chapel was not in the plans, but by some miracle a huge aching hole in each other's heart was being filled.

The fall was coming on and I sat on Jimmy's famous patio nursing a beer, while he jabbered on about the terrific deal he had gotten on a European Viking Cruise on the Blue Danube. In fact, he and

Catherine were scheduled to fly to Amsterdam in a few weeks. To hear him tell it she was as excited as a high school girl before the prom. She and John had always wanted to visit Europe but had never quite gotten there before he died. It all sounded great to me.

I just couldn't resist, "Jimmy, if I didn't know better I might think you are whipped over that woman."

He gradually turned his head and looked directly at me trying valiantly to summon a look of indignation at my suggestion, but he quickly turned away when he couldn't suppress his grin, "Nah. She's just a friend. Someone to talk to."

Sure, Jimmy. Sure.

We paused for a moment, totally relaxed and lost in our own thoughts. Suddenly our reverie was interrupted by a loud bleating siren. An EMS ambulance rumbled by Jimmy's house with flashing lights blazing. We both sat up with concern. Based on the direction the vehicle was headed it had to be for one of our neighbors. Jimmy looked over at me with a panicked and stricken look and whispered one word, "Catherine".

When we arrived at Clear Lake Hospital, she had been taken into emergency surgery. We never saw her but did notice several hospital attendants rushing about. My wife and another neighbor arrived a few minutes later. We all sat in that horrible stark antiseptic waiting room for what seemed like hours without any news. Jimmy was a total wreck. All he could say was "I didn't even get to say goodbye," as tears streaked down his cheeks. We tried our best to console him, but what could we say?

Finally, a young man with a "Dr. Patel" name tag on his green scrubs appeared from behind the swinging doors. His report was terse and to the point. Catherine had suffered a massive stroke. The next twenty-four hours would be critical, but, frankly, he wasn't optimistic. Jimmy collapsed on to one of those plastic chairs and buried his head in his hands. He sobbed for a few minutes and then swallowed hard. "I guess it was just too soon," he mumbled. "With Annie gone I had no right to ignore her memory the way I did." We endeavored to reassure him that Annie would not have minded, but he was not to be convinced.

Almost before our eyes we watched this grand and ebullient man retreat back into darkness and gloom.

A week went by. There was no change in Catherine's condition. She remained uncommunicative in a coma, virtually on life support. There was some discussion about pulling the plug, but no one had the authority or would have been inclined to do so. I visited Jimmy every day, and my wife and other neighbors brought meals in, none of which he ever seemed to touch. He had very little to say, other than inquiring about Catherine's condition, which had not changed.

It was a Sunday morning, and I stopped over to see him after church. I was surprised to find that he had shaved and smiled as he let me in. He looked a lot better, and we even talked a little Texans football. He ate the bagel I brought him and sipped a cup of coffee. Based on the way he'd been lately he was in unusually good spirits that morning. He almost beamed at me with a wide smile as he said goodbye when I let myself out. My wife was heartened by the news. Maybe he was finally coming around.

I had been parked in front of the TV for a good part of the afternoon watching the Texans-Packers game, when a horrible thought struck me. I jumped up and searched on the mantel for the extra key to Jimmy's house. I rushed out the door and ran across the lawn to his front door. I was too late. He lay there in bed looking quite composed and serene. The EMT's simply could not bring him back from all the pills he had consumed. Why, why, why hadn't I recognized the signs when I was there that morning? There was one short note in his neat hand writing on a yellow legal pad next to the bed

"I have now lost two. I simply cannot go on any more."

Oddly enough, Jimmy turned out to be wrong. As miraculous as it seemed, Catherine pulled out of it and made virtually a full recovery. When told of Jimmy's passing, tears welled up in her still sparkling eyes. She sat there quietly for a moment, but then dug deep for a smile.

"I will miss him very, very much. We had a nice thing going, but I always knew I was only renting him for a while. He belonged to Annie. I hope she is not too cross with me. At least now they are together.

I suppose it won't be to very long until I show up. Then maybe Jimmy, Annie, John, and I can have a drink just like old times."

"Til then, I need to get over to the mall and pick up a few things. There's that movie I want to see. And, oh yes, the HOA board. I almost forgot about it."

PANNER'S FINAL PROBLEM

Aaron Ward

JERRY DID NOT make it into San Antonio often, but there were plenty of things he would rather do in the city than go antiquing. Still, he kept his sigh internal as he allowed his petite girlfriend, Meisha, to pull him past an aluminum and glass door of a strip mall antique shop he did not even read the name of. The space next to it was a dry cleaner, and on the other side, a yogurt shop.

Once inside, the air-conditioned interior wrapped him in a cocoon of cool comfort, strict relief from the blazing summer heat. Meisha's small, manicured hand let go of his larger, calloused one, and he took a moment to enjoy watching her walk in her pink tank top and jean shorts, her blonde ponytail waving back and forth across her back. He was over a head taller than Meisha, with a dark tan complexion and a full head of black hair. His years of playing football gave him broad shoulders and legs like pillars, but she could pull him almost anywhere.

Shelves and cabinets filled the space with just enough room for two people to walk past each other, stuffed with anything large enough to hold a price tag. Jerry grinned at the chaotic variety of old knick-knacks, curiosities, and shelf stuffers to bring home and converse over. The smell of wood polish mixed with a faint trace of sweet smoke hung in the air. The store was more expansive on the inside than it first seemed, and the pair wove through the miniature maze of items.

As the door softly closed behind them it muffled the sounds of traffic from the busy street.

The couple was only in the city for the day, hunting for this very shop and a specific bracelet Meisha had seen on their website. She had told Jerry of the bracelet repeatedly, how it looked exactly like one stolen from her grandmother, and it might be the same one. The theft occurred two years ago, and the plan was to purchase it today.

Jerry fully supported the trip and the sentiment behind it, but preferred rural areas to urban life. The long winding roads of central Texas appealed to him far more than the clogged arteries of San Antonio, and the shade of buildings did not cool him as well as the reaching branches of a developed tree. He pushed his sweaty dark hair out of his eyes, and thought about sitting with a nice cold drink in the shade. After this chore was over he was sure he could convince Meisha to go for a swim in the pool.

She led him to the back to find the shop keeper, a sour faced man with receding grey hair and stubble on his cheeks to match the bushy mustache over his lip. He was wearing a red checkered short sleeve shirt over his stocky frame, and sweat shone on his hairy arms. He was perched on a stool behind a glass counter with clear shelves scattered with jewelry, and more shelves surrounded him, smothered in smaller objects and figurines. The old man let a smile quirk his lips when she walked up.

Jerry pumped his moist grey tee-shirt against his chest while he browsed the closely grouped merchandise, and Meisha inquired about the bracelet. The assortment of items would have impressed him if he had not been in shops just like this before. These dusty relics were saved from estate sales and junk piles, the slightly valuable refuse of a disposable society. They served only for nostalgia now.

His slow steps took him to the back-right corner, a poorly lit area. He liked to explore the corners and hardest to reach places in shops. It interested him to look at things people rarely bought or thought about. Out of place among the shelves, a plastic folding table held a collection of rocks and geodes displayed with their colorful crystals facing each other. In the center was the largest rock, black, rough, and as big as his head. Extending from the side of the black rock was something that looked like it belonged on the set of a science fiction movie. It was oblong, tapered at one end, and made of smooth silver metal. On the top was a segmented bulb, and to Jerry it looked like part of a face of some mechanical insect. He could see no tool marks, rust, or other imperfections on the dull metal, and he reached to touch the segmented eye.

When his skin contacted the silver surface an image of the entire metal face flashed through his mind. The segmented, bulbous eyes sat on top, and the head tapered to two mandibles closed in a straight line.

With a deep breath Jerry took a step back, feeling a sense of dread and fear that came with the image. He knew what happened. Sometimes when he touched things he got flashes, memories, attached to the item. It was how he knew his brother had taken his truck without asking last summer, and how he knew his high school girlfriend had cheated on him. Touching the handle of his truck had given him a flash of his brother's exuberant face behind the wheel, and touching his ex-girlfriend Louise's necklace gave him an unwelcome sight of her arms wrapped around the running back from his old team. Other moments that his 'gift' showed him were much shorter, and often he was unable to make out anything clearly. It was not something he had control over, and sometimes it would go months or over a year before it happened. Now this metal fragment had something to show him, something he had never seen before. Jerry steadied his nerves, and touched the face again.

It was not merely a flash this time, and Jerry looked with terrified eyes at a pair of robot drones facing him. The shop was gone, although he could still recall being there, and the sounds, smells, and sights around him were as real as the bustling Texas street he had been walking down only minutes before. Despite his awareness he felt like a passenger, a witness with no control over what happened, and he knew things that he did not before, like that the thin metallic automatons before him were called drones. Their articulate limbs with narrow pointed fingers carried long metal bars, shock sticks, that could expel enough energy to cook him, but they were not ordered to kill him unless he attacked or tried to escape. Not long ago he stood before a tribunal of judges passing down their verdict of guilty for dereliction of duty. His crime was that while he was engaged in unofficial war games, the sector under his protection was attacked and six colonies were wiped out. They sentenced him to exile currently being carried out by the drones.

Behind the mechanical enforcers his lifelong rival stood, gloating with fists on his hips. His white hair tinged with grey stood up from his skull in a curving wave, and his long blue face held a smug sneer. A flash of silver escaped his long dark blue lips from his metal teeth, and his diamond shaped pink eyes glinted in amusement over his broad hump of a nose with narrow nostrils. He was wearing a bright green uniform with a yellow belt of tassels around his waist, and his gloves were of matching yellow. Each of the tassels was a rank of authority. This was Nokrus, the man he hated most in the galaxy, and behind him was the only way off this judge-forsaken world. Nokrus' shuttle was a thing of beauty, a half-blue, half-green sphere with a silver band of lights around the center, dividing the two colors. The hatch was open, bright with the comforts of civilization, and the walkway was still lowered with his vile rival standing at the bottom.

"The judges decided not to execute you, Panner," Nokrus said, "but no one will find you out here. Wait until you meet the natives. It's quite the barbaric scene."

After being called by name a wave of new information flooded through Jerry's mind. He was looking through the eyes of Precipitous Panner the Nineteenth, formerly a war hero, but now disgraced. From the way the blue being's lips moved Jerry could tell he was not speaking any language from Earth, but he knew the meaning. He continued to witness, entranced as Panner's eyes flicked to his surroundings, weather beaten rocks with green topped trees and a scattering of weeds, ground coated with whatever happened to grow. The rough terrain culminated in towering snowcapped peaks in the distance, and somewhere far off he heard rushing water. Overhead was a pale blue sky with a glaring yellow sun and stringy white clouds.

Although the setting was familiar and comforting to Jerry, he could feel fear and revulsion from his host over what he considered a hostile alien landscape.

Panner tensed his body, ready to implement his advantage. On the journey inside the ship he was held with restraints, capable of only a slow walk and no use of his arms. The restraints were woven fibers on his forearms and ankles lined with sensors that took commands from the ship to be as tight or loose as desired. Normally the restraints would be turned off after the ship departed, and in this climate, would degrade quickly. However, he felt the restraints go slack as soon as he left the landing ramp. He could not imagine what had done this, some malfunction or possible environmental effect, but it did not matter. This was his chance to escape, and he would rather die than be stuck on this spinning mud ball. He was Panner the Nineteenth, commander of the Savage Fifth Fleet of the Ocius Empire. A legion of space cruisers once obeyed his every command, and he would not spend his last few decades huddled in cold, rocky places hunting and squatting like a primitive. Images flashed through Jerry's mind of strange, spiked ships spinning across the sea of stars, glowing with their own light. Their movements did not follow anything he recognized of proper physics.

Panner slipped free of his arm restraints and leapt forward, grabbed the rod of the right drone, and pushed it up into the face of the one next to it. As programmed the drone electrified the rod to force him to release it, and he did, leaving most of the power scorching through the brain of its partner. As the stricken robot toppled Panner grabbed the rod from its limp grip, and swung it into the side of the head of the first drone. The construct lost its footing and slipped down to one knee, but Panner was already running past it. Cursing, Nokrus ran back for the shuttle and reached it ahead of him, screaming for the autopilot to take off. Panner leapt through the hatch as it slid closed, rolling to his feet.

The inside of the shuttle was lined with leather made from an extinct species of canine, purple and gleaming in the overhead lights of the ship. The floor of the craft was black tiles lined with gold trim.

To Panner's right was the control panel with three empty seats. The shuttle was programmed to respond to Nokrus' verbal commands, and the panel was there for emergencies. He could use it to pilot the vessel, but only if Nokrus was not there to counter his directions.

His formerly gloating rival bared his silver teeth, but it was just a show to hide his fear. Panner was really a prisoner of the drones, and his enemy's presence was merely tolerated. What was not tolerated was for Nokrus to have any weapon or defense device with him, nothing that could interfere with the drones performing their duty. He was practically naked in that silly uniform. Panner hefted the shock stick and hopped towards him, the restraints on his legs active once more. He could not use the rod's offensive blasts, but it served well as a cudgel. The next images flashed through Jerry's mind too quickly to comprehend, but he knew that Panner won the struggle. Although Nokrus commanded a rival fleet, he was at heart a politician, and his indigo blood splattered the walls by the time his body stopped moving. Jerry could taste the taint of blood in the air, and it almost made him break contact. He persisted, though, fascinated by this barbaric being from a more advanced civilization.

Panner discarded his gory weapon, and was thrown against the wall as the ship lurched. The shuttle was attempting to fulfill the final order of its master and return to the cruiser in orbit on the other side of this planets moon. That was normally a smooth trip, but Panner was still the prisoner of the drone on the surface. It was programmed to do anything to keep him from escaping, including shooting down the shuttle regardless of who was on board. Another blast from the drone's shock stick rocked the ship, throwing Panner into Nokrus' still warm corpse.

He sputtered against the bitter blood splattered over his face, and did his best to roll away from the body as the ship shuddered a final long time. The internal suppression systems kept crashes from being fatal for the occupants, and for the shuttle to react that way it must have smashed into something hard. Panner let out a long sigh as he stared at the inactive view screen of the shuttle. Once the cruiser lost signal with the transport it would leave without sending a rescue mission. Nokrus knew that and took the risk to have his last chance to gloat. Panner the Nineteenth was stuck in whatever corner of the galaxy his enemy had chosen, and all records of the trip would be erased. His family and allies, still somewhere in the great expanse fighting for the glory of the Ocius Empire, would forever wonder at his final fate.

With the ship disabled, the restraints still on his ankles came loose, and he tugged them off over his narrow blue feet. He triggered the manual switch for the entry hatch, which lurched halfway open, and climbed out of the vehicle. The ship had smashed into a long outcropping of stone, teetering on the edge of a narrow canyon. Far below a river roared white over jutting orange rocks, twisting and turning on its natural course. Panner saw that if some of the rocks came loose, the shuttle would topple into the canyon. Some trees nearby had been clipped by the shuttle, their branches torn free and scattered, and so it was easy to find a suitable lever. He set it to the ship and heaved, sending the vehicle on its final trip, and was satisfied with the loud crunch that the vessel made when it hit bottom. The rushing water quickly carried the mangled shuttle away, and Panner spit over the edge as parting sentiment for the last resting place of Nokrus.

Panner heard his final problem approaching through the shattered trees, battering aside any vegetation in its way. The drone could track him by sight, scent, or sound, and could confirm his biological readings with samples on file in its memory. The thing's sensors had a range of miles, and there was no way he could escape it, not that he would try. Yet, he would not stand still and simply let the thing shoot him either, so he ducked back behind a large rock and waited. The smooth motions of the drone were silent, but its footsteps drew near. Panner took a rock in his fist and flung it over his head towards the sound before rushing around the other side of the rock. The drone was ready for him and fired, sending searing pain shooting through his leg. Panner's momentum carried him and the slight machine over the edge as he planned. They toppled and Panner pushed at the face of the drone, determined to fight to the end, and felt the impact when the battling pair fell onto the first rock.

Panner knew it was his death blow, unable to will his broken body to struggle as he slipped into the river. He could not breath, could not feel his heart beat, but the last thing he saw was his hand extended from the water holding the decapitated head of the drone.

Jerry took another breath and stepped back. Meisha was standing beside him, smiling, holding her arm up to show him an ornate silver bracelet with opals and sapphires.

With clear pride on her face, she said, "It's the same one. It's even got the scratch on the underside from where her dog grabbed it. Granny is gonna flip." She must have seen something in his face as she added, "Are you ok?"

He grinned. "Yeah." He turned back to look at the rock and the half-drone face. Gripping it by the rough part he lifted it and saw $20.00 on a red tag adhered to the underside.

Meisha gave him her curious look. "You gonna buy that? What're you gonna do with it?"

Jerry replied, "See if there's another half of a face underneath the rock." He carried it carefully up to the counter to pay the man his money.

Why I Wrote This Story

Panner's Final Problem is a fictional story about a man exploring his ability to relive memories attached to objects. I got the idea from being in antique stores and wondering about the previous owners of the items. I took the story to the extreme level of using a prehistoric memory from an extraterrestrial mind imprinted onto a robot's severed head. I wanted to contrast the extraterrestrials advanced technology against their human-like behavior towards envy, rivalry, and violence.

ALL IN GOOD TIME

Larry Morris

JERRY WALKED INTO the cafeteria and started toward the table occupied by his coworkers. As soon as he crossed the threshold, he felt he had been here before. Not in the cafeteria; he had been in the cafeteria hundreds of times. He felt as if he had been here, on this day at this time, before. It was a very odd feeling. He stood just inside the threshold for a few moments trying to think about how he felt. Frustrated, he shook his head a little and proceeded to his coworker's table.

He sat down and listened to the conversation. Jerry was Dr. Jerry Tillison, operations director of the new BHR-10, a black hole reactor. He was very good at what he did, but he had no idea how this reactor actually worked. It had something to do with creating microscopic black holes and harnessing their power to control a self-sustaining fusion reaction. The only person who actually understood its inner workings was Dr. Madison Stills, its creator. The only problem was, he died weeks before the reactor was turned on for the first time. Jerry didn't like not knowing what it actually did; he liked it even less when he found out he was the person who had to turn it on. He was, of course, capable of managing its operation, he knew how to run the damn thing, a reactor was a reactor. But he hated not knowing how it actually worked.

Brad and Anna, two of the reactor's senior technicians, were arguing.

"I still say it's dangerous," Brad said. "None of us know what's inside that damn thing and how it really works. I think it's dangerous."

"You said that already, Brad," Anna said. "Just do your job and quit whining."

"None of us know much about how the reactor really works," Jerry said. "Perhaps we should just stop arguing about it and get back to work."

"You would say that," Brad said. "You're part of the establishment."

Jerry ignored the remark, and they all sat in silence for a full 10 minutes. Just as Jerry was about to say something else, everything got fuzzy; it was like things were rushing away from him. Then the world just went black.

*   *   *

Jerry walked into the cafeteria and started toward the table occupied by his coworkers. As soon as he crossed the threshold, he felt he had been here before.

He stopped just inside the threshold. This was more than just déjà vu. He sat down at the first available table, empty at the time, and thought about what was happening. He even remembered the conversation he had been part of at the other table. How many times had he done this? Was he caught in some kind of time loop? Before he could think of what to do next everything got fuzzy again; then the world just went black.

*   *   *

It took Jerry several dozen trips through the loop to decide he really was in a loop. He seemed to be the only one who recognized the whole world was in a time loop. It took him scores of trips through the loop to develop a plan to get out of it. The biggest problem was that the loop only lasted 15 minutes. Fifteen minutes right on the nose, every time. He had to turn the reactor off; as far as he was concerned that was the only option. It was causing this time loop, he was sure of it. He struggled with whether to try to explain the situation to Brad and Anna. He couldn't say just why, but he knew he would need their help to turn it off. In the end he decided to tell them and enlist their help.

He began by using the next several trips through the loop to formulate what he would say. He had to formulate it in his head. If he wrote it down anywhere it wouldn't be there the next time through the loop. Once he knew what he was going to say, he would start writing on the cafeteria wall as soon as he got there. The wall right next to Brad and Anna was white and had nothing hanging on it.

It took dozens more trips and patient practice to be able to write his whole explanation on the wall in under four or five minutes; every time through the loop the writing, and everything else he did, disappeared. After several iterations of reading Jerry's explanation on the wall, Brad and Anna began to realize they were part of a time loop with Jerry and the rest of the world. Jerry never did figure out why he was the first one to recognize the anomaly; he thought perhaps it was because he was the one who started the whole process by pressing the *start* button on the reactor.

On the next several iterations of the loop, they discussed what should be done. Of course, they had the discussion after reading and understanding what Jerry had written on the wall.

"So," Brad said, "you think we should just turn the damn thing off." It was more a statement than a question.

"Yes, that's exactly what I think," Jerry said. "We can't go on living the same 15 minutes over and over again."

"A really short version of *Groundhog Day*," Anna said and laughed.

"What the hell does Groundhog Day have to do with what's happening here?" Jerry asked.

"*Groundhog Day*, the movie," Anna said. "You need to get out more. But I agree. We can't just not do anything."

"Okay," Jerry said. "The only real issue is the reactor is in the basement of the office building and we keep popping up here in the cafeteria for the 15-minute loop. I'm not sure we can get to the office building, get to the basement and turn off the reactor in under 15 minutes. Realizing, of course, that we have to go through everything in one iteration. Reading what I write on the wall, understanding it, having this very conversation again, and then getting to the reactor and shutting it down. All in under 15 minutes."

"That's not the worst thing," Brad said. "There ain't no *we* in this. From my limited understanding of how the reactor operates, the real kicker is that there is a significant delay between pushing the *stop* button and the black holes dissipating. If they dissipate at all. That means whoever does this will most likely get sucked into one or more of them. It ain't gonna be me."

"I remember reading at least that much," Jerry said. "It wasn't intentional, it just had to do with the time it took for them to dissipate. So I'm the only one who's going?"

"No," Anna said. "I'll go with you." Brad shot her an ugly glance.

"Don't come running to me when you get sucked up in one of those black holes," Brad said.

Anna ignored him. "If we're going to do this, let's start on the next iteration of the loop. There's no telling how many times it will take us to get there."

All of this discussion and planning actually took place over 18 iterations of the loop. For a while they kept getting stuck on Groundhog Day. When they were ready to go, they headed for the office building right after the last set of conversations.

There were people milling about all over the place outside and this slowed them down the next few iterations. Some of the people invariably wanted to try to start a conversation with one or both of them. These poor souls had no idea what was going on, just living the same 15 minutes over and over again.

*   *   *

It took about a dozen or so iterations to get them to the reactor building in under three minutes. Jerry was impressed, he had no idea he was in such good shape. They used another six or so iterations discussing exactly who was going to do what when they got into the building.

Anna was going to run interference for Jerry and he was going to turn the reactor off.

Neither of them really knew what to expect when they got in the building, let alone in the reactor room. Anna went in first with Jerry close behind. It took them a full 30 iterations just to get to the basement. Between security guards, scientists ambling along reading instead of watching where they were going and not knowing where the stairs were. They had a lot to cope with. The elevator was restricted, so they had to find the stairs, then it turned out they were locked. They figured out how to snag a set of keys from a guard they passed to get through the basement door.

It was Dungeons and Dragons all over again.

Once they had everything down pat, they had 30 seconds left when they skidded into the reactor room. Realizing, of course, that every time through the loop they read Jerry's explanation on the wall in the cafeteria, had several discussions, decided to make their way to the office building, avoided people and traffic on the way and had the final discussion about what to do when they actually got in the building. Every. Damn. Time.

As soon as they arrived at the reactor, they could feel the pull of the black holes. The only way they could shut it down was to make a human chain to reach the *stop* button. Anna held onto the door jamb with one hand and one of Jerry's hands with her other. They both stretched out as far as they could and Jerry tried to reach the *stop* button with his free hand. He couldn't quite make it.

With about 10 seconds left, he let go of Anna's hand, lurched forward and slammed the *stop* button. He could hear machinery winding down as the reactor finally came to a stop. At the same time, he felt himself being pulled inexorably toward the reactor chamber and the black holes.

He noticed from the clock on the wall that they had exceeded the 15 minutes by several seconds. It had worked. Whatever happened, it would be worth it to just get out of this damned loop. Even if he had no idea what was going to happen to him. He saw Anna waving to him as he was pulled into the reactor chamber. The black holes were shrinking, but they still had enough attraction to pull him in. The last thing he remembered was that it had been Brad who helped him the last time.

*   *   *

The sun hit Jerry's eyes at just the right angle to rouse him out of a light sleep. He had been dreaming about something exciting, but had lost it as soon as he woke up. He hated that; he didn't even have the chance to write it down. He got out of bed and shuffled into the bathroom to get started on his morning routine.

Today was a big day and something was already nagging at him. Something at the back of his mind that he knew he should remember and take into account. Since Dr. Stills had passed away, he was the man in charge of the reactor. He had yet to go through all the material Dr. Stills had left, that would take months and he didn't have that kind of time right now. They wanted power and this new reactor was their only option anymore. Fossil fuels were all but exhausted and wind and solar were still not efficient enough for all their needs. Clean, cheap fusion power had to be their salvation.

Something still nagged at him. One of those things where you knew you were supposed to remember something and couldn't. It would be right on the tip of your tongue all day and never quite solidify. It was annoying.

Today, all he had to do was stand at the reactor console and push a button. With millions of people watching on live TV. No pressure.

He got to the BHR-10 complex by 8:30. The ceremony wasn't until 9:30 but he had a couple of people he needed to see first. He made his way to his office building and up to his small office. He dropped his briefcase on his desk and crossed the hallway to Brad's office. As he expected, Anna was there, and they were trading stories about the night before. They stiffened when Jerry came in.

"Do either of you have any misgivings about today?" Jerry asked.

"You mean other than the fact that this is a damn crazy idea?" Brad said.

"Yes," Jerry said. "Besides that. I have the funniest feeling. I've had it since I got up this morning. Something I can't quite put my finger on that I should remember."

"No," Anna said. "Nothing like that. Just the same objections we've always had. Don't turn it on, Jerry."

"We don't really have a choice," Jerry said. "If I could just remember what it is that I have forgotten. Unless you can offer me a concrete reason not to, it's going on in," Jerry looked at his watch, "twenty minutes."

He left Brad's office and made his way down to the basement and the reactor room. Cameras and microphones were set up all around the control console, and media people were everywhere. He took his spot in front of the console and waited.

The announcer went though a monologue Jerry wasn't really listening to. He was looking at the console. There was the *start* button right in front of him, and right next to it was the *stop* button. He looked at the *stop* button and knew there was something he was supposed to remember but still couldn't.

When the announcer got to the right spot in his monologue he pointed to Jerry, and Jerry reached down and pressed the *start* button. The world went black.

*   *   *

Jerry walked into the cafeteria and started toward the table occupied by his coworkers. As soon as he crossed the threshold, he felt he had been here before. Not in the cafeteria; he had been in the cafeteria hundreds of times. He felt as if he had been here, on this day at this time, before. It was a very odd feeling.

Why I Wrote This Story

Groundhog Day was one of my all-time favorite movies, a masterpiece of the maddening, frustrating ever-repeating situations that's still hilarious today. I thought, how about combining my favorite subject material, science fiction, and a Groundhog Day situation, where the characters were actually trying to save the world?

THE FORGOTTEN

Jan Sikes

A COLD WIND HOWLS across the thick dark purple expanse of the Egluna star. Its ferocity, farther north, increases driving the furred ones to seek cover, and the two-leggeds to huddle like a grove of trees leaning into a storm.

Thirty-nine moons have passed since our suns broke through the thick barrier that shrouds our granite star. The evidence is seen in every direction. The heavy skin of our people, the Eglunites, is chalky. Eyes are dulled and hope dead.

We have long ago stopped dreaming of anything more, accepting the dark fate that has befallen us. We are nothing short of walking dead, going through the motions of bleak daily existence ... no feeling, no light, no belief.

We are the forgotten.

That is how he found us on the day of his arrival. Hurtled through an invisible portal, he falls with a thud bellowing, "Xander," that resounds throughout our tiny desolate planetoid. And despite his turbulent arrival, he alights with grace beyond anything we've ever seen. Both feet easily planted, his translucent ebony skin glistens and his Peridot green eyes shine with light, something foreign to us Eglunites.

He towers over us, a good eight feet or more. A beautiful creature, he glides as though his huge feet never touch our parched gray ground. And while he doesn't speak words, we are drawn to him in an inexplicable way.

"Who is he, and what is this strange power he possesses?" We scratch our heads and whisper amongst ourselves, lest he hear us.

He then turns to fully gaze upon us, and we see it. He is a Fresh One. It has been written about, eons ago, on our granite tablets but we've never witnessed such a being. Not in our generation or the generation before.

He has powers! His eyes like golden green beacons shine bright. But, it is when he looks with the 'One Eye,' that things miraculously begin to change.

He gives his attention first to our dying plant life. Almost immediately, it starts to take on moisture as if awakening from a terminal drought. The leaves slowly uncurl and stretch in a long drawn out yawn.

We watch him from afar and marvel. Then a distant memory of a way of life long abandoned vexes our minds. Slowly, awareness begins to awaken from its deep slumber, much like the plants, except at a slower pace. It resembles the gradual uncoiling of a sleeping serpent.

The two-leggeds gather in small groups, speaking in hushed tones. Then an elder suggests that we experiment with using our own 'Eye.' Afraid and ashamed of failure, we practice at first in secret.

With our nine suns no longer visible, we can only mark time by the changes in our moon. It's hard to tell a day from a night or how many have passed.

However, we guess it to be approximately 3 moon-days, hours, minutes and seconds later that Companion arrives. She drops through the same portal, her landing less graceful than the one Xander had executed. Tumbling head over heels across the rocky terrain, she comes to rest against a large boulder that cracks in half with the force of her impact. In two moon-seconds, he kneels beside her, offering his hand and righting her to stand.

For a long lunar moment, their golden eyes lock and we are forced to turn away from the brilliance. But, only moon-seconds pass before we are drawn back. Through their ebony translucent skin, we witness two hearts beating as one and see them large and full, transferring energy.

We gape, mouths open, at the exchange. It is almost as if we are witnessing a sacred and private union. And yet, they make no attempt to hide, so we make no attempt to look away.

Her skin, unlike his, glimmers with a hint of purple and her long flowing hair looks as if it's been spun of pure gold. Also, unlike him, she stands only a little over seven feet in height. But, her eyes—those golden beacons shine exactly as do his.

Why have they chosen our desolate planet to fall into? For whatever reason, the weary Eglunites welcome the distraction.

With two Fresh Ones on our drab gray star, things begin to change. Slowly, bit-by-bit, as we witness the miracles they bring with them, the two-leggeds begin to awaken from a forever dark and hopeless slumber.

The furred ones curiously approach Xander and Companion, sniffing and twitching their long black tails. When either reach down to touch them, transformation happens. Their fur coats are no longer dull and lifeless. They glisten and romp through the boulders with energy anew, always running back to rub against the legs of the Fresh Ones or lick their huge thick feet.

My Egluna brothers and I explore the tablets on which the ancient ones recorded the powerful phenomena of The Fresh, long before we came into existence. Words, foreign words, like hope, joy, and love slowly take on new meaning. We've not experienced, nor truly believed, such wondrous things ever existed, despite what our history proclaims.

Our practice to reopen The Eye in each of us expands into group sessions facilitated by Xander and Companion. As if teaching a child how to walk, they gently prod and encourage. In one session, Xander reaches into a large canvas bag and brings forth brightly colored fruits unlike any we've ever seen. He passes them out to the group and waits while we turn them over in our hands before he speaks. Funny, how his mouth never seems to move but he communicates with a perfection that leaves no questions.

"Taste them," he commands.

I sniff my piece of fruit before opening my parched mouth and biting down. As the juice flows across my tongue and trickles down my throat, I am quite sure I've never tasted anything so sweet, so delicious.

My fellow Eglunites each follow suit. And then something quite unexpected happens. Our hearts, shriveled from the long night of darkness, take on life again. They expand inside our chests and glow ever so slightly. We gaze upon each other and feel a stirring. It is just as our ancestors recorded.

Moon-days go by and our godforsaken star begins to revive and renew itself.

Then out of the blue, the heavy dark shroud, that has lain for so long across our home, parts and there they are. Our nine suns! They warm us all the way from the tops of our elongated heads to our pointed toes and linger to rejuvenate 'The Eye' and the heart with streams of energy direct from Source.

We stand in a large circle with arms outstretched. My chalky gray skin tingles and glows ever so subtly. I stare in amazement at my planet family. Never have I witnessed such beauty. After some time, we all take on a rose-pink color that shimmers in the healing rays.

I have a companion, as do other Eglunites, but those memories are long buried. As I gaze at her now, I call her name. Sarondish turns and smiles. Slowly, she comes into my arms. With her head lying soft against my chest, pleasure fills me. A stirring in my groin brings back even more obliterated memories.

Then something else rises slowly from the core of my being. Hope for life better than I've known springs forward. Hope for renewal, regeneration, and replenishing.

As the suns continue to transfer life force energy to us, the forgotten ones, a surge comes. At first, it is barely noticeable. Then it grows and fills me from the inside. It is exactly what we've read about on the granite tablets left by the Ancients.

Our ancestors called it joy. I begin to dance! Other Eglunites join me. We hug. We even smile so big it eventually turns into a laugh.

Each of us can now fully see through the One Eye and it glows with life and Fresh energy.

For days, nights and weeks we indulge in this new-found life of laughter and love.

We've all but forgotten Xander and Companion. When we notice their absence, panic strikes.

Fearful murmurings can be heard amongst us. "Where were they?" They can't leave. We need them.

And then, as if on cue, Xander stands tall and shining while Companion's brilliant aura blends exquisitely with his.

"Our job is done here," Xander thunders. "You must not forget. You must look upon your Suns daily and keep The Eye open. Source is pleased with you and will smile favorably on you so long as you don't forget."

With that, they exit, hands joined, back through the portal from where they first came.

They'd brought Fresh energy allowing us remembrance. Now, it was up to us to keep it alive and well.

Gazing with love and gratitude at our flourishing habitat we cry in unison. "We promise to never forget!"

We then carve new granite tablets to make sure when we are the ancient ones the new will always remember.

For as long as we live, laugh and love under the energy rays of our nine suns, Source and The Fresh stays renewed inside our hearts.

Egluna, the tiny radiant star twinkles and thrives in the galaxy still, all because of Xander, Companion, and Source who chose to smile upon us.

Never again will we be the forgotten ones.

The End

Why I Wrote This Story

This story came to me at three o'clock one morning and I had to get up out of bed and write it. It is parallel to the way I view society as a whole in present time. Walking dead, unfeeling, unseeing beings, we are desperately in need of the Light.

PLAIN BROWN WRAPPER

Mark Allen

THE OLD MAN loved his garden.

He grew colorful flowers in beds surrounding his home and vegetables and other leafy plants in a hothouse.

At the moment, he worked on a flowerbed, preparing the soil for the coming fall and planting bulbs for spring. Sometimes he would spend the entire day planting, pruning and pulling weeds, stopping only when his wife would interrupt him with a cold glass of lemonade.

Then, came her illness.

It took seven months for the cancer to take her. She tried to live as she always had the first few months, going too often to the stupid church down the street. She'd said she wanted to spend her last days on earth helping those in need. It hurt them both too much for him to complain about her devotion to the church or those dingbat churchies.

He'd doted on her as best he could, never coming close to the attention she had shown him throughout their marriage. She died on the sixth day of the sixth month, after 60 years of marriage.

He visited her grave every day, complaining as much as he had when she was alive.

"That stupid nurse," he'd ranted on his last visit, "Always showing up at the wrong time, always late, always slow to make you comfortable. I should have fired her."

The headstone always listened patiently to his rants.

"Another one of those dingbat churchies came by the house the other day," he'd complained. "'We're so sorry for your loss. We're all praying for you.' Like that's supposed to help?"

He'd glared up at the sky, "And where were you? She busted her butt going to church, cooking food, teaching bible classes to the churchie brats! And for what? She's gone! And I'm all alone!"

And so on.

The old man stood up from the flower bed. He was thirsty, so he went inside and poured a glass of lemonade from the pitcher in the fridge. He took a long sip, making a face, hating the taste of powdered mix. He poured it down the sink. Putting the pitcher away, he saw his grocery list under the magnet on the door. It was time to go to the store.

He changed out of his gardening clothes, putting on a pair of slacks and a buttoned shirt, slipping his bare feet into his loafers. He drove to a store that was only a few blocks from his house. As he drove home, he passed the small church his wife had attended.

On a whim, he steered the car into the parking lot and stopped near the front entrance. He stepped out of his car and gave the building a long, disgusted look.

All the time she'd spent here, he thought. What a waste.

"Can I help you with something?" a voice asked politely.

The old man was startled by a younger man sitting in an SUV beside him.

"Uh, no," the old man stammered. "I guess I'm a little lost," he said. It was the first thing that popped into his head. Strange.

"Well," the younger man said, "I'd be happy to . . ."

"No, I'm fine," the old man said. He didn't want a sermon. He zipped out of the parking lot and headed home. Back in his house, he stood at the kitchen counter to catch his breath. What was wrong with him? He'd talked to the churchies before. Why was he so rattled?

He needed to calm down, so he put away the groceries and changed into gardening clothes. Minutes later he kneeled in the backyard, preparing the flower bed for bulb planting. He was focused and breathing evenly.

"Um...hello," a voice said.

He jumped, turned around and glared at the person who'd startled him so badly. It was a little girl, about 10 years old, dressed as little girls did these days.

"You scared the heck outta me!" he complained. "Where'd you come from?"

The girl pointed to the open gate. He'd been in such a hurry when he'd come in with the groceries, he'd forgotten to latch it.

"I didn't hear you come in," he said.

"Sorry."

"Why are you here?" the old man asked. "You a stalker or something?"

"I'm eleven," she said, frowning, "I'm not a stalker."

The old man's voice was gruff, "So why are you here, then? Selling cookies? Magazine subscriptions? What?"

His sudden interrogation scared her.

"No, I . . . I'm here to help you . . . I . . . I . . . ," the tears began to form, her voice quivering.

"Okay, okay, calm down," the old man said, trying to stem the sudden flow of emotions he didn't want to deal with. "Stop with the waterworks."

The girl stifled her tears, sniffling.

The old man turned to the flower bed, "You're sure you're not here to garden?" he asked sarcastically.

The girl didn't respond but watched him work with interest. She seemed to be making a decision.

"Dingbat," the old man muttered under his breath.

"Okay," the girl said, laying her package aside. She dropped to her knees beside him, "Show me what to do."

The old man was alarmed. "What? No, I don't have time to . . ."

"Like this?" the girl asked, picking up a spade and digging in the soil, "Is this how you do it?"

"No, no . . ." the old man took the spade from her, and then saw the disappointment in her eyes, like a puppy who'd just been scolded. He sighed, giving in, not wanting to see more tears. He demonstrated how to use the spade,

"Like this."

The girl mimicked his actions when the old man handed her the spade.

"Am I doing it right?"

"Yes," the old man said. He watched her work, removing the weeds, culling the soil. He grabbed an extra spade from his caddy. He began digging alongside the girl.

After a little while, the old man brought out the Dutch iris bulbs and showed her how to plant them. It took an hour to plant them all. By the time they were done, the old man was talking all about gardening. He offered the girl lemonade, pointing out the iron garden bench while he went inside to pour them both a glass from the pitcher in his fridge.

"My favorite are the daffodils," he said as he handed her the cool drink and sat beside her on the bench, "They're beautiful when they come out in the spring."

"Pretty," the girl said, sipping. She liked the coolness of the drink on the warm day. The old man drank his own, making a face.

"This is instant lemonade. I don't much care for the aftertaste," he paused, reminiscing, "My wife used to make it fresh-squeezed," he said.

"It was great," the girl agreed.

"You knew my wife?" he asked.

The girl nodded and handed the man a package. "I came here to give this to you," she said.

The old man turned the package around in his hands. It was wrapped in plain brown paper, tied in twine.

"Open it," the girl prompted.

He tore the paper and saw an aged, leather-bound book that he instantly recognized. It was a bible.

But it wasn't just any bible. The faded gold lettering on the bottom of the face was a name he recognized, "This was my wife's," he whispered.

"My Sunday school teacher," the girl said, sad that the old lady was gone. They all loved her.

The old man flipped through the pages. Many were worn and tattered.

"I wanted to get her a new one, but she said she couldn't give this one up. There are notes and underlines all through this thing."

"She really knew her bible," the girl said.

He saw a common note in the margin and read it aloud: "Pray for him."

"Yeah," the little girl said.

"Hello?" a woman's voice called out from the side yard, through the open gate. "Is anyone there? Hello?"

"Uh, oh," the old man said.

"Who is that?" the girl asked.

"Some churchie lady who keeps bringing me food," he told her. "The dingbat doesn't know how to take no for an answer." He smiled at the girl, "She may be trying to poison me."

The girl gasped, hoping he was joking.

"Hello?" the voice called again.

"In the backyard!" the old man yelled.

The woman's head appeared at the open gate, seeing the old man and little girl. She stepped into the yard. She was carrying a clear container full of cookies.

"Well, hello!" she said, overly animated.

"Hi," the little girl said, recognizing her from church.

"Here again?" the old man said rudely.

"Well, uh, yes," the woman stammered. She held out her container, "I brought you some cookies. Oatmeal chocolate chip."

The old man glanced at the little girl, "Do we like oatmeal chocolate chip cookies?"

The girl nodded, smiling.

The old man accepted the cookies, "We like oatmeal chocolate chip cookies," he said, "My friend and I will share them."

"Oh, good," the woman said, pleased she'd managed to find something the old man would finally take.

"Thanks for stopping by," the old man said, nodding at the gate behind her. He had to glance at the gate a second time before the woman caught his hint.

"Well, okay," she said, leaving. "Have a nice day, you two."

"Stupid dingbat," the old man muttered when she'd gone.

The little girl was incensed.

"Why are you always so mean to people who are just trying to help?" she asked angrily.

"Mean? How am I mean?"

"Calling everyone 'dingbat' and 'churchie' all the time! Being mean to that lady who made you cookies! Yelling at little kids like me!"

The old man was indignant.

"I didn't ask you to come here, kiddo, and I never asked for anyone to bring me food." He set aside the cookies. "And I sure won't put up with some brat judging me in my own back yard. So you can..."

The girl jumped up, "Is is four o'clock yet?"

The action startled the old man, diffusing his anger. He glanced at his watch.

"Almost."

"I did what I came here to do then," the girl said, stomping across the yard toward the open gate.

The old man was stunned by how quick they'd gone from being friendly to unpleasant, "Wait!" he said.

The girl paused, looking back at him impatiently.

"I have another flower bed to plant," he said, trying to mend their argument, "Want to help tomorrow?"

The girl shook her head. "Thanks for the lemonade."

She left quickly. The old man glanced at the bible in his hands and finished his drink.

Several days later, the old man was sweeping his front sidewalk. The neighborhood was quiet. He hoped to see the little girl again, tell her he was sorry and ask her to help him plant flowers. But she never came by.

The next day, the old man stopped by the church. When he stepped inside, he was in a small foyer leading to the sanctuary. Some books were on a shelf along one wall. A poster or two decorated another. When his eyes fell on a framed picture hanging on the opposite wall, he froze.

It was a picture of his wife.

He stepped over to it and read the brass nameplate attached to the bottom of the frame. It had her name and "Beloved Friend and Faith Warrior" below it.

"Can I help you?"

The old man stepped back from the picture, startled, and turned. It was the same man he'd seen in the parking lot days before.

"Uh, yes," the old man said. "I was looking for a little girl. She came by the other day and helped me plant some flowers."

"Can you describe her?"

The old man did, from what he remembered about her.

"That describes about half the kids in our congregation," the other man said. "Maybe come by on Sunday. You can see if she's here."

The "no" look on the old man's face was easy to read.

"Well, I don't think we can help beyond that," the younger man said, nodding to the framed photo. "I saw you were admiring this."

"Yes," the old man said, his eyes softening. "She must've been an important person."

"She was a good friend to everyone," the younger man said. "We lost her to cancer a few weeks ago. Her Sunday school class wanted to honor her, so they had her photo framed. We put it out here so we could all remember her."

"What's 'faith warrior' mean?"

"She didn't just say she was a Christian. She acted like one, too," the other man said. "She cared for others, spoke boldly about her faith and prayed for those who needed it." The younger man paused, reminiscing. "She used to say the most wonderful prayers. Heartfelt."

The old man felt a twinge of grief. "Didn't seem to do much good, though, did it?"

"What do you mean?"

"She died anyway, after all the praying."

"Oh, she never prayed for herself," the man said. "We did that. She'd pray for others. Children, newlyweds, others who might be sick," he paused. "She prayed for her husband every day."

"Really?" the old man said, looking at the photo.

"Yes. I understand he's not a believer. She'd always hoped he'd come around someday."

"You know," the old man explained, "Fire and brimstone, devils and angels. Churchie."

"Oh, I see," the younger man said. "Well, I guess that's the whole point of us being here. You know, the church. All of us are trying to give someone else the chance to go to heaven."

"By learning more about God," the old man said, beginning to understand, glancing at the picture. She'd told him about it many times when she was alive, and he'd taken it for granted she'd be around forever. "And now, she's in heaven," the old man murmured.

"Yeah," the younger man said.

The old man took one last look at the picture on the wall, and headed for the exit.

"Will we be seeing you on Sunday?" the younger man asked. The echoing "thud" of the door was the answer.

After supper, the old man read the newspaper for the second time. When he couldn't sleep, he'd go over the pages of the paper again, in case he missed anything or to read the obits to see if he knew anyone he could brag about outliving. He finished it a second time, just before midnight.

And yet, he still wasn't sleepy.

Beside him, a smaller version of the picture hanging inside the church sat on the table at the end of the couch. He'd laid her bible next to it, a small shrine to the woman who'd loved him all these years.

He reached for the bible and flipped it open and began reading her notes once more. He hoped that something inside would explain the life his wife had led outside of their home. He read passages she'd underlined beside the "pray for him" note in the margin.

When he woke up to the sound of birds singing outside his front window, he realized he'd fallen asleep on the couch. The bible lay open in his lap, still turned to the page he'd been reading. Something about forgiveness. He recalled a decision he'd made during the night that got him off the couch and into the shower.

After dressing in a suit he hadn't worn for years, he drove to the cemetery. Standing at her grave, he felt differently than the last time he'd visited. The bitterness wasn't there, as it had been most mornings since she'd died.

He closed his eyes and thought of the perfect bond they shared. It must be like that, he thought, being close to God. I hope you are happy in heaven, sweetie, and that you are with friends and family, he thought. I will see you again someday.

He left the cemetery and drove to the one place he never thought he would. The parking lot had a few stray cars, so he was able to park close to the entrance.

When he entered the foyer, he stopped to look at the photo on the wall and felt a love in his heart he hadn't felt since she'd first gotten sick.

Then the old man made his way down the aisle of the empty sanctuary. Halfway to the front, he slid into one of the pews and allowed himself to absorb everything around him.

"You missed our services today," a voice said. The younger man he'd met in the foyer walked toward him.

"Won't be the first time," the old man replied. "I'm getting on in years." He sighed, looking around the room, enjoying the quiet coolness. "Is it okay if I just sit here for a little while?"

The younger man nodded. "We've been saving a seat for you for years, sir. Welcome."

Out in the foyer, the girl who'd given the old man the bible eyed the photo of her Sunday school teacher who'd taught her so much about people.

"Pray for him," she said, watching the old man talking to her minister. She smiled, knowing this prayer had been answered.

Why I Wrote This Story

Mark Allen originally wrote, directed and edited "Plain Brown Wrapper" as a film short. He based the main character on his father. A media instructor/missionary adored by students around the world and a supporter of Texas Authors, Mark wanted to enter the Short Story contest this year and adapted his screenplay for it. Sadly, Mark died unexpectedly June 17. So his tale of a mourning spouse missing a person beloved by all takes on new meaning.

THE HIGHWAY CHAIR

Julie B Cosgrove

I DON'T QUITE UNDERSTAND how I got here. I recall a bump, and then I wobbled until another bump catapulted me over the rail. Thunk.

I tipped over backwards and rolled down the hill, landing upright by some bizarre quirk of gravity. And now here I sit with the buzz of traffic whipping against my sides. A sharp ache crawls up my spine from being whacked several times as I tumbled.

Everything is blurry.

I think part of me is missing.

My skirt is torn.

Someone, please stop and help me. I may be old, but I could still be useful.

Come on. Don't zip by. Back up, get out, and look me over. See if I can be fixed up.

I wait. The day lingers. The sun beats down on me.

The cars just zoom past. No one cares.

Please, this is not the way I want it to end . . .

*   *   *

I remember my delivery day. Yes, I absolutely do. Brand new, fresh and smelling wonderful. Quite a cute one, if I do say so myself.

Sure, there were hundreds similar to me made that year, but I think

I stood out. Maybe it was my color—harvest gold. Very popular in 1968. Not too long after they released me from the plastic wrap and wheeled me out to the showroom, a nice young couple bought me.

Jim and Jocelyn. Yep. Those were their names. I will never forget them. Jocelyn was about to have their first baby and Jim thought an upholstered rocking chair would make her life easier. I recall her clasping one hand over her heart as the other stroked across me—her touch softer than my fabric. Love eked through her fingers and sent a chill through my frame.

Water dripped from her eyes onto my arms as she eased into my soft cushion. The liquid felt surprisingly warm. At first I worried she might have leaked, which would mean they'd probably throw her away. Jim apologized to the salesman that she broke down like that, yet she seemed fine to me. Jocelyn would leak a lot from her eyes that first year. I later heard women with babies do that sort of thing.

With two quick rocks, Jim helped her up and they gave the salesman money. Two men lifted me into the bed of their truck and off I went to my new home, the wind whistling through my springs. My pride soared. I belonged to someone. And in less than four hours of being displayed on the showroom floor, too.

The couple placed me in a room with a box on legs. They called it a changing table. I'd never seen anything like it before. That weekend she rocked in me and tried to read a piece of paper, which she kept rustling and refolding as Jim sat on the floor creating a crib from pieces scattered across it. He never uttered a word, but his face would become red now and then.

Two months later another face appeared. A very tiny one. It often turned red as well. That's how I knew it must belong to Jim. The resemblance, you see. And loud? Oh, my. That doesn't begin to describe the wails that blasted from its mouth. But it also had a soft gurgling coo that soothed my heart. They named it Joey. Sometimes Jocelyn would hum or sing as she rocked Joey.

He leaked, too. But not always from his eyes. Guess people do that. Little wonder with all the liquids they drink.

After Joey grew bigger, he'd sit on her lap as she read stories. I loved those times because I could listen, too. Her voice rivaled the birdsong outside the window.

Joey's legs became stronger and longer. He often climbed into me. He would bounce and throw his weight against my back to make me rock. I tried to help out because I knew it made him giggle. Joey had a wonderful laugh.

After two years, they moved me down the hall to what they called the den. Another box lived in that room along with a leather chair called "Easy." When Jim and Jocelyn came in the room to sit down, they would click on the box. It would begin to glow and make wonderful sounds and pictures. Voices, music and nature scenes emitted out of it—sometimes quiet, other times loud. The box made them happy, so I liked it, too.

I stayed in that room for several years. One day Joey spilled grape juice all over me. Jocelyn scolded him, sent him to his room, and then scrubbed me down so hard it hurt. She cried as she did it, but I don't think it was because I looked ugly, all purplish yellow. Eventually most of the stain came out. One spot toward the back seam of my cushion never quite vanished. They hid it with a small pillow.

I stayed with Jim and Jocelyn for nineteen more years. They had two other children, Jamie and Jesse, who loved to be rocked in me as well. Those kids crawled all over me as they chased each other. I can still hear their laughter. I never told them their shoes hurt.

One by one the boys left the house. I guess they grew too big and tall. The house became very quiet.

Then, Jim took me outside. I sat on concrete along with other items. Chairs, tables, old toys, and various household items surrounded me as people weaved in and out. Some punched me to see if I felt soft. I didn't mind. My cushions had been pressed in and thumped a bunch over the years. I'd gotten used to it.

A woman bought me and Jim helped load me into her van. My sides scraped as they angled me in, but with a few tugs and grunts, I eventually fit. It hurt to be jostled with my sides pressed like that against the metal, especially when we went over holes in the street or around curves.

At last the vehicle stopped and another group of hands tugged me out. They carried me into a little gray house with blue shutters. It smelled like lemon wax and cinnamon . . . and something else old and musty. A gray-haired woman with a sweet, wrinkled smile told them to set me near a window. She brushed me down with her hands and rocked in me. Her voice shook but it still contained an almost melodious tone. "Yes, dear. I like this very much. Thank you."

The woman who purchased me gave her a hug and called her Granny. Other people who visited her referred to her as Irene. She often hummed like Jocelyn had, but to different tunes. And she'd knit for hours on end as she gently rocked back and forth. Sometimes she laid a warm pad at my back. She told me it helped her sciatica, whatever that is.

Irene sat in me for fourteen years. Then one day she didn't get up. Her body became cold, heavier than usual, and very still. The woman who bought me came to visit two days later and wailed louder than Joey, Jamie or Jesse ever did. It broke my heart.

One more time men loaded me into the back of a truck along with Irene's couch and other things. I went to a place called a shelter. For twelve more years many different people sat in me. They came and they went. Men, women, young, old. Some slept in me. Many didn't smell very good. A few threw up on me. But I rocked for all of them. It's what I was made to do, after all.

Then, two days ago a huge man sat in me. Oh, how he strained my fabric. I heard the creak, and then part of my frame gave way. Crack! Off he tumbled.

I couldn't help it. I am old, you know. They no longer let me stay there. They carried me to the curb. I sat in the sun for two days wondering who my next family would be. I got used to the pain.

Once again men lifted me into a back of a truck, but this time they wedged me on top of stinky trash and twigs. Until the vehicle hit one those bumps and I tumbled out. That had never happened before. It shocked me.

*   *   *

And now, here I am by the side of a busy highway. Guess no one cares to sit in me anymore. I have been here for close to a week. Abandoned.

Today, the sun has disappeared. Now I hear rumbles. Rain. I know that's what is coming but I've never felt it before. Only seen it and heard it pelt against the windows in the places I've lived. It patters on me—cold, damp and sharp. My fabric becomes soaked. I shiver.

Nobody will want me now. How useless I feel.

Something tugs at my skirt. A small grayish animal with whiskers and a fluffy tail scurries under it, followed by her three babies—two gray like their momma and one yellow. Hey, the same color as me when I was new. I wonder, will it fade as it ages like I did?

They cuddle between my four legs. Soon, I hear a soft whirring sound. Rhythmic, steady. Then a few tiny mews jitter my old springs as her children settle and nurse, safe and dry. I remember that smacking sound. Jocelyn's boys used to make it.

Somehow, knowing that I'm keeping them dry makes me care less that I am getting drenched. I've served others all my life. Almost fifty years. It's what I do.

Perhaps, just perhaps, I am still useful after all.

The mother and her kittens live under me for several days, but then they move on. Who will need me next? A buzzard perches on me, waiting no doubt for small animals to be squashed by the cars. I've seen several of them die that way. Eventually he flies away.

Another week passes, during which two more rain storms saturate me. But nothing takes shelter under my skirt. The grass grows up and tickles my rockers, though.

Wait. Here comes a huge truck. Men with bright orange vests jump out and lift me. They swing me back and forth and let go. I sail into the top of the truck and land on . . . oh, no.

Trash bags and twigs again. I jostle inside for hours as they stop, grab more unwanted items along the side of the road, and toss them on top of me. Finally the vehicle slows down, and backs up with an ear piercing series of beeps. I feel the top end rising and . . . whoa.

I slide out the back and land on top of more trash. Stinky stuff. It disturbs a myriad of flies. They buzz and land on me. Yuck.

So this is home now? Am I to rot here, alone and unwanted? Peeking through the bundles of bags and tree limbs I see other sticks of furniture. Also an old refrigerator, tires, and some of those TV boxes with cracked or broken glass. I've never felt so distressed in my life. I can't even move to rock.

I can't do what I was designed to do. And I stink.

*　　*　　*

Three weeks go by. Then I hear voices and a man pulls me out of the heap. He flips me over and shakes my broken frame. Ouch.

I hear him say, "I'll give you twenty bucks."

He and the owner of the junkyard toss me into, yep—you guessed it. A truck. Off we go. I don't want to get my hopes up, but a smile eases across my fabric. I won't miss the flies, roaches, or the stench.

He takes me into a garage and sets me on a table. Then he begins to rip my upholstery away. Hey, stop that.

Each tug pops out more staples. I try not to scream. He couldn't hear me anyway. Humans never have been able to.

Now I'm naked. The man shuts off the light, closes the workshop door, and leaves me in the dark—shivering, bare. I have never felt more humiliated and exposed in my life. Oh, dear. What's next? Can life get any crueler?

I wish I could leak from the eyes like the humans do. It always seemed to make them feel better. Wait, I don't have eyes. Oh, well.

Four days later my new owner returns with sacks. He begins to rub my frame down with sandpaper. In a way it feels rather good. I had developed a few itches around the holes left by the staples. Next, the man sets my break with glue and a few nails. Yes, it hurts as he pounds them in, but my hope begins to revive. I think they call this being repaired.

The next day, white fluffy stuff is wrapped around my back and arms. He staples it on with loud bangs and pops, but the pricks tickle more than cause pain. New foam is fitted for my cushion. Then he drapes me in the prettiest fabric I'd ever seen. It is striped in pastel colors but it has flowers as well. It takes the man two more days to finish my renovation. He stands back, nods with a smile, and loads me into the bed of the truck again.

Where are we going? Surely not back to the dump . . .

We arrive at a brick house. A young couple hurries to meet us. When she sees me, the woman squeals as she bounces up and down on her toes. They carry me inside and place me in a room. She sits in me, rubs her hands over my arms and softly cries. Could it be?

I gaze around the room. Stuffed animals, fluffy curtains in the same colors as me, and a crib share the space. That confirms it. A new human life is coming.

And life for me will continue. My heart swells. I almost sense a tear emerging.

Now, I know why sometimes my owners weep. It's out of pure joy.

Why I Wrote This Story

For weeks, as I commuted to work, I passed a dilapidated, harvest gold chair on the shoulder of the highway. Not something you see every day. It intrigued me. How did it get there? Who had sat in it over the years? If only it could talk . . .

Then one day it was gone. I'll never know what happened to it, so I decided to write a story about it. And of course it had to have a happy ending.

I hope my highway chair's did as well.

We all have a purpose, no matter our age, physical condition or talents. Never think you are not useful to others, you are. Your life has meaning.

NEVER ON FRIDAY

Kenneth E Ingle

SIX A.M. FRIDAY the hospital was ready. Everything seemed fast paced yet practiced. These people had done this before. A nurse appeared and said she'd be with me throughout the operation. Asked which hip the surgeon was to replace, I said the right one. She nodded and put a blue mark on the target and then gave me a knockout drug and off we went.

The next thing I remembered was in the wake-up room and it was three p.m. everything as expected. Iv's in my arm, attendants awaiting my wakeup and hospital type paraphernalia crowded the room. Alert, it took a few seconds to get my bearings. Fortunately, the painkiller hadn't worn off. Actually, even after four hours in the operating room, you'd think pain with a bit of moaning was the norm. I felt very good considering I'd been under the knife and saw.

The swarm of young attendants surrounded me, and without malice or prejudice, I can say there wasn't a born American in the bunch. The aides were cheery and helped with anything I needed. A young Filipino did everything he could to make the large plastic slab taped securely in place comfortable. It separated my legs and kept them immobile and everything in place.

A pleasant but all businesswoman appeared in the doorway, clipboard tightly clasp. "You have to be out of here by five. It's four fifteen now," she said in a practiced voice meant to convey her intension. "Where do you go for rehab? Here or somewhere else? If you stay here, it will cost one thousand dollars each day. We can arrange financing." There was no sorrow or humor, no emotion just facts.

Before I could answer, my surgeon (unnamed although he did a great job) entered. By then, my son and daughter were also in the room.

"All that was taken care of over two weeks ago," the surgeon said.

"The insurance company says there were mistakes on the application, and it was returned to the doctor's office," unrelenting the business voice said and added gazing indifferent at me, "Your carrier has not given authorization for any rehab."

"Always blame the doctor," said my surgeon nonplussed to say the least. Apparently, unable to contribute beyond his only remark, he vanished.

Bless cellphones. My daughter made a call to the insurer and sure enough, no care authorized beyond surgery and that the insured would have to resubmit the request for consideration. It shouldn't take more than two weeks.

I later learned that this was an oft-used tactic. Seems the insurers hope you'll give up and do your rehab at home where they won't have to pay or, at the least, fork out less. I live alone so going home wasn't an option.

Panic in spades. Again, thank goodness for cell phones. A marathon of calls began with no success. Finally, I had my daughter call the VA (Veteran's Administration) and they offered to provide transportation, and rehab at their hospital with the understanding they would charge my carrier. Not a problem for me. This information my daughter forwarded to the insurance company, and amazingly they immediately found a place for my rehab. At five minutes to five, the lady with the clipboard handed me a list of medications, along with one day's supply, as an orderly loaded me onto a gurney and minutes later into an ambulance. It was one minute after five.

I must tell you about a young African aide at the hospital. She had a smile and manner that could conquer Troy. During one of

our exchanges, I asked how she liked it here in America. Her answer
stunned me. "I love being here and taking care of you rich Americans."
Now believe me I'm as far from rich as any person can be and still not
be on the dole.

A missionary found her in a Uganda refugee camp. I suspect her
alert mind, personality, and smile got her plucked out of that terrible
place and schooled at the mission; then on to the U.S. for nurse
training and possibly more. She had left a life without family, without
hope, without the means for survival. Misery and death were her
constant companions. It's easy to understand why she would see all
Americans as rich. How damned fortunate we are.

We arrived at the rehab center, at the back door, around five fifteen.
There was no one to meet us so the ambulance driver put me in the
first room that had an empty bed. My kids left to their own families.

An orderly arrived to tend my roommate, and she took a few
moments to tuck me into bed. Things started to settle down. By six
p.m., meals wheeled up and down the hallway. The servers ignored
my pleas for food.

The building had four wings, mine seemed quiet, and without the
antiseptic aroma experienced when visiting non-ambulatory rehabs
locations.

An aide reappeared and I asked about my roommate. She shook
her head, came near my bed, and whispered, "Mr. Smith isn't doing
very well. They doubt he'll make it." That did nothing to raise my
spirits. Again, she listened to my plea for food. Same response: "I'll
tell my supervisor."

It's reasonable to assume just my presence, ensconced in a room,
unable to fend for myself, would result in some recognition; like
another mouth to feed, this guy can't walk, bedpans needed and what
all. Moreover, I still had two needles stuck in my arm trickling fluid in
and a catheter trickling fluid out.

At seven p.m., a call to a passing aide, I asked for food not having
eaten since noon the previous day. The young lady said, "You aren't
assigned to me. I'll see if I can find who's working your room."

By eight p.m., the specter of starvation arose and had no appeal.

Since nothing else worked, war seemed the only course. With my call light ignored (since no one had been assigned to me), a yell to another aided passing down the hallway nailed him and my demanded to be fed—forcefully stated. Thirty minutes later and no response, everything reachable flew into the hallway. Bedpans make a noise even on a carpeted floor and that seemed to work.

A cook showed up with a raft of papers, thumbed through them and with a smile, she said, "Man you came in at the worst time possible. The full-time staff went home at five and you got here after they left. No one checked you in and the regular staff won't be back 'til Monday morning. There isn't any fixed dinners left but I'll put something together for you." With a giant smile, she marched from my room. I had made progress. Starvation seemed distant.

The day shift personnel were the only true employees of the rehab center. The exception, the charge nurse, and the person who dispensed medications. All others, evening and weekend, are contract labor.

The lady from the dining room reappeared and said she'd added my name to her list, wagged her finger, and added, "I'm going home but that will get you breakfast. Now, you have to tell the morning cook to add your name for Saturday, Sunday, and Monday. Then the regular staff will be here and you can be fed like everyone else." At nine p.m., I finally had the most delicious food.

Sound like the problems solved? The day started without breakfast and I had to scrap for every meal. A few questions and I learned the oncoming staff never bothered to check for messages. I fought all weekend for every morsel. By Monday, the battle was joined and me still bedridden. Occasionally, an aide would take care of the bedpan. I wasn't rude, but demanding, yes! It Didn't help a bit. For the rest of my stay, I was the last fed. Some of the helpers knew about me and saw that I had food. I still hadn't made the *to be fed* list. On a number of occasions, I had to get out of bed (after I became ambulatory) and steal a tray from the rack. Understand, the off-hour help, as contract labor, seldom the same people showed for work two days in a row. The day shift crew, when told of my problem, had a stock answer: I'll tell my supervisor. Nothing changed.

The charge nurse and the one who dispensed the drugs were the last to check in a patient. The administrators are first, the center being able to collect for any service rendered is most important. Anyhow, the medical nurses, being last, always file their paperwork. Therefore, the people who make up the various lists had no record of my arrival. Someone told the bookkeeper I was there, so the billing stuff was in order and to the bean counters, the world was right. I still wasn't on the anyone's list, and I had to daily scrounge for food, gowns, bed linen, wash cloths, toilet paper and wheelchair; broken I add, which I repaired to usefulness. By then, the rehab nurse had come to my room and arranged to start that phase of rehabilitation. She pulled out the plastic slab, the one immobilizing my hips and legs, and handed me crutches. "Get up. I'll help you and from now on, keep moving. I want you up more than down."

This rehab center wasn't anything like I had expected. First, it was remarkably quiet. All the floors had carpeting and there wasn't the anticipated aroma associated with medicines and sick people.

Mr. Smith, my roommate, was something else. He wasn't doing well. Acute renal failure, a missed diagnosis. Renal poisoning destroys muscle tissue so Smith needed physical therapy in an attempt to forestall further deterioration.

But Smith had *it*; whatever *it* is. The guy had a manner about him that you just had to like. The women attendants couldn't keep their hands off him. Combed his hair, straightened pillows, helped him dress, played cards, anything the guy needed, they were there. I would say to him, "Smith, what is it with you and these women?" His wife, a lovely lady, enjoyed the teasing, and I was as relentless as envious. This guy got coffee brought to him in bed, rehab, recreation room and I couldn't get a crumb.

Twelve thirty one morning Smith wasn't feeling well. He'd had his call light on for almost an hour. I punched mine, dozed off and on. About four a.m., no one had come to help as he lay in his own filth. Smith was a big man; six-foot seven, his wife six-five, and he was in a diaper. As I said, there were no odors—great ventilation. I yelled as at a man passing down the hallway. That brought him and a nurse from the station. Smith got the care he needed. The guy who was supposed to be working our area had taken off and the charge nurse hadn't noticed.

I was sleeping about four hours a night so the staff was accustomed to my roaming around the place in a wheel chair or on crutches. This was my scouting time, and I checked the call light register at the nurse's station and could see it was functioning properly.

When Smith's wife learned what had happened, she was ready to skin someone. However, neither of the Smith's wanted to cause a stir. I told her to think about it. If she needed a willing advocate, I was ready. By that afternoon, she had decided to say something and let me know. Yet, it took two days for Mrs. Smith and me to get an audience with the administrator. Smith was now up and around going as he pleased. He was everywhere except wanted no part of the confrontation. A card table, set up at the end of the hall drew the cardboard shufflers. And of course, Smith was there to the ladies glee. Women were three deep waiting for their chance to get into the games and you could hear the moans when he had to leave. I convinced it was that *it factor* again.

Mrs. Smith and I presented our concerns to the administrator; her husband's lack of treatment and I used the opportunity to give *my not on anyone's list* including getting a bath. The administrator apologized and said we needed to supply the names of the offenders. I wanted tell her the complete personnel roster should about cover it. But I didn't. Instead, Mrs. Smith pointed out all the aides and staff always turn their ID badges over so no names are visible. The administrator raised her hand to protest then realized she wasn't wearing her nameplate. Mark one down for the good guys! She let us know Mr. Smith had only to press the button at his pillow and a nurse would respond; unless the board wasn't working properly. I informed her of my nightly jaunts and that Smith's light was on which I pointed out to the charge nurse. Mark two for the good guys.

Hearing of my dastardly reception, the administrator said she'd check into it. Didn't help. Nothing changed.

About one a.m., up making my rounds, I found the wheelchair off in a remote spot broken, and abandoned. I spotted the problem and fixed it gaining mobility. Each night I wheeled up and down the aisles always under the charge nurse's suspicious glare. Then the first salvo came my way. It seems no one had authorized a wheelchair for my use. I reminded her I still wasn't on the food list, had to get my own bed linen and bathed in the lavatory. She stomped from my room. Smith laughed and that only aggravated the situation. A few days later, the charge nurse said I'd have to give up the wheelchair.

That night, as I slept, someone took the wheelchair. The next night, on crutches, I spotted *my* wheelchair sitting in a hallway. Whomever was using it didn't understand how to manage the 'fix' I'd made. Again, I restored it to usability. Hefting the crutches, I wheeled back to my room. From then on, I removed the repair placing the needed part under my pillow. The chair was mine!

Rehab went well. A drill sergeant ran that end of the business and she wouldn't tolerate any slothfulness. She'd heard about a new patient but had no papers and came looking on her own. She knew it was vital my rehab start immediately. Blood clots are a major enemy and the only remedy is immediate exercise. And she worked my butt off. It's a good thing I stay in shape. I go to the gym at six times a week and this really helped my recovery. She said my response to her regimen was better than she had ever seen.

Smith got better and went home two days before my discharge. That day my admission papers arrived and I got my first real bath. The lavatory remained a fond memory.

It came time for me to go home. The physical therapist came to my room. She said, "I must tell you, the way you treated Mr. Smith probably had more to do with his recovery than anything we did here."

Even in my cobbled up wheelchair, I felt good.

SUPEREROGATE PARK

Aaron Ward

A FTER THE FOURTH time telling the boys not to run in the house, and the first time of my wife giving me her 'Do something with them' look, my two sons and I headed out to our favorite outdoor place to play. Supererogate Park, located only a few short blocks from our modest home, was a typical public park stocked with swing sets, jungle gyms, and one average sized merry-go-round, all made of smooth, rounded metal with plastic covers on anyplace a little skull might collide with. The various surfaces were painted in bright colors of blue, yellow, and red, interchanged to the point where no one would be confused that these choices were absolutely intentional.

Our city had put some money into Supererogate Park. The parking lot was level with straight yellow markings for appropriate spots with thin shrubs at the border. Beyond the cement the grass was trimmed along with the darker green bushes that lined the walls of the brown brick community center facing the lot. To the left were tennis and basketball courts, flat concrete slabs divided into the sections where fit people either whacked or bounced their balls. Aluminum benches lined the outside for observers, and a high chain-link fence kept the action safely contained.

We walked past the community center and beyond that was a wide field of grass cut across with cement walkways for joggers, mothers pushing strollers, or dogs walking their owners. On the other side of the field was the playground, already teeming with activity. Towering pine trees surrounding the play area granted patches of shade, and a layer of bark that looked like it could have been peeled off the nearby trees covered the ground where any child might fall.

The sun was shining on a warm February afternoon in south Texas, and the congregation of strangers assembled at the park was simultaneously familiar and unwelcoming. When it was my time to play as a child in this park, a couple decades ago, conversation between consenting adults was the familiar backdrop, but my sons live in the era of instant communication. I could see the seated parents and guardians like outcasts from the fun, staring into their hand-held screens with blank expressions, occasionally looking up to make sure no molesters were closing in on their little ones.

My boys, Chester and Travis, six and four, ran ahead of me, and the oldest, Chester, looked back grinning over his shoulder to shout his customary challenge, "Catch me if you can, Daddy."

"Yeah, chase us," encouraged Travis, his chubby legs quickly losing ground to his longer brother's.

My protruding gut and spindly legs could tell anyone that I was no athlete, but despite the reproaches from my body I lurched after them across the grass towards the playground. I always chase them, because each passing day brings my children closer to the moment when they will say those words for the last time. Their maturing brains will hit silent, hidden switches deep within, and their thoughts will turn away forever from the simple joys of racing their father to the more complex diversions of approaching adulthood. Knowing that, I don't want to look back and say I passed up even a single chance to run with my boys.

I did not have to pretend to fall behind Chester. My six-year-old had already outpaced me, but I could still play the game with Travis. I ran behind him, letting him win, and watching his brown curly hair bounce as he made his way brought a smile to my face. I had dressed him in a green tee-shirt with a fashionable action robot on the front with blue jeans. The green shirt would make him easier to find in the throng of perpetually moving children. Chester was in a grey tee-shirt and cargo shorts, his choices.

The excitement was already well under way. Children darted in all directions, whiffing down slides or crawling up them, kicking their legs in squeaking chain swings or waiting their turn with expectant expressions. The thick plastic of the climbing areas allowed for a variety of holds and grips interspersed with metal bars and poles for little arms to propel developing bodies. Surrounding it all was the thin layer of adults, and I quietly took my anonymous place among them.

The contrast between the parents and children always caught my notice at Supererogate Park. The young ones could have been plucked from all over the world. Their skin colors ran from light to dark, their features amalgams of descendants from numerous continents. For the girls hair styles ranged from free flowing long locks to tightly bound tails and twists, straight or curly, black to blonde. The boys' hair was all short but differed in the same way. The clothes were likewise a combination of options. The boys were in tee-shirts and jeans of diverse styles. A few of the girls wore shirts and jeans as well, but also sensible blouses with skirts and flip-flops with plastic jewels on the thongs. The playmakers ran every which way without time for hierarchies or discrimination, while their reasonably attentive guardians sat in self-segregated groups. I straightened my glasses and smoothed my blue polo shirt over my gut as I headed to the gazebo for a place to sit. I passed by one white couple to sit between an asian pair on my left and a line of black ladies on my right. No one noticed my quiet rebellion.

While Travis was busy crawling over the jungle-gym's proportioned to his size, Chester had landed at the merry-go-round. Grabbing one of the glossy yellow handle bars, low at the rim and higher toward the center, he planted his white sneakers firmly on the circular red bottom perforated with diamond shapes. I did not bother to count, but there seemed a dozen other children clinging to the yellow bars, spinning in mirth and defying the centrifugal forces. The riders were such an adequate complement of diversity that if I saw them in a commercial I would guess they had been chosen for that purpose. One little boy in a blue shirt with short curly hair sat facing the edge, his skinny legs tucked under him, and with a silver pouch of juice in his hand. A yellow straw made the connection from pouch to mouth. A couple of girls sat close together, their resemblance clear, and with the larger one's arm wrapped around the younger. A boy and girl sat on the edge chatting with each other and letting their legs dangle in the trench formed in the dirt from countless pounding feet. Others stood like Chester, and the moving array of arms and legs made a dizzying display.

As the merry-go-round began to slow an unexpected drama formed before my eyes. When it became too sluggish half the children hopped off, some to find other enjoyment, but others like Chester held onto the yellow handle bars and pushed their legs into the trench to reinvigorate the spin. Working with one purpose the children made the merry-go-round turn. The boy with the blue shirt did not move from his seat, the straw never leaving his mouth. Of the sisters, the larger one got up to help, but seemed more intent on the younger girl than her efforts. She quickly reclaimed her place, holding both arms around the smaller girl this time. The boy and girl on the edge let their feet drag in the trench with mischievous grins, clouds of dust rising as they hampered the work of the others. Despite the discord the pushers outnumbered the draggers and the merry-go-round began to spin quickly again. The children regained their spots to enjoy the ride.

Other children ran up, some jumping on with practiced ease, others hesitating and staring at the turning yellow bars like the jaws of some threatening beast. The merry-go-round slowed again and the process repeated with fewer children helping to push, although I was happy to see my son still giving effort. The feet draggers continued their opposition and the device spun slower and with much shorter duration. The smiles of the riders began to wilt.

One of the oldest boys stood up and turned a disapproving eye on his peers. "We should all get down and push," he said, finishing with a laugh that told of his disbelief that he had to bring up such an obvious detail.

Urged by his example, most of the children jumped off. The feet draggers abandoned their contentious game and left to find another. The older sister hopped down but strayed no farther from the younger. The boy in the blue shirt still did not move, and the yellow straw stayed stuck to his lips.

With more of the players helping the merry-go-round took its fastest turn yet, obligating the boy in blue to hang on to one of the yellow bars to keep from falling over. When it had reached acceptable speed, the children leapt back on to enjoy their efforts, but soon it began to slow again.

One of the fathers, urged by his son and inexperienced to the ways of the merry-go-round stepped up with a broad grin. I quietly predicted disaster as he cheerfully told the children to hang on, gripped one of the yellow bars and pushed with his adult might. Faster and faster he spun it, grabbing and shoving a new bar as it became available to his meaty hand. The force overwhelmed the entwined sisters, and they attempted to abandon the ride, landing in the dirt with much crying and sadness.

I shook my head and realized the humble merry-go-round had shown me a short example of how our society works. It only keeps going when pushed, and some are happy to help knowing the ride is better for it. Some are content to sit and allow others to work for them, sipping incessantly at their chosen brews. Others take their enjoyment in hampering the efforts of the group, smirking while they ride and drag their feet at the same time. Leadership can help move things along, especially in times of inadequate activity, but leaders can only do so much. Then sometimes a well-meaning idiot with more brawn than brains shuffles over and really shakes things up, thrilling some and endangering others.

My son abandoned the large toy with its complicated metaphor and scampered over. "Let's go try the swings," he said before running off.

I smiled and followed.

Why I Wrote This Story

Supererogate Park is based on an actual event I witnessed at a public park in Beaumont, Texas. I changed the personal details of myself and the children I was with, but the interactions between the kids on the merry-go-round are all accurate and unprompted. Even as I watched the little drama unfold I knew it would be a good scene for a story. I am not the adult at the end that spun the toy too fast and sent the two girls into the dirt. I already learned years before to let the children push themselves.

BEE IN THE CAR

Curt Locklear

FIRST OF ALL, I'm allergic to bees. That's very important to this story. I carry an epinephrine pen with me wherever I go, because a bee sting could cause me to kick the bucket. Lucky me. Secondly, my neighbor called me a wimp because I couldn't lift a tree limb that had fallen in my yard. Not anything I'm proud of, but I would probably be featured on the "Lives of the Wimpy and Not Famous" TV show. I've come to grips with that and try to live my life in my own limp, deflated way, avoiding controversy wherever I can.

My story begins on a sunshiny day. Fluffy clouds floated above me as I drove along a peaceful country road. I rolled down the window to feel the cool breeze and smell the wild flowers and do all that communicating with nature that I have heard that we are all supposed to do from time to time. The sun was, well . . . warm. The birds were soaring, and, besides the flowers, the roadkill was smelling. I felt fully connected to nature.

Being in such a state of euphoria and in no particular hurry, I was not bothered at all to see the sheriff's car parked by a field of sunflowers, clocking speeders.

As fate would have it, (and you know how fate is. It's never nice. It just gives you a wedgie and laughs in your face.) just as I passed the sheriff's car, a bee flew in my window, hovered right in front of my eyes, sizing me up to see if I was a good enough sting victim to die for—a tough decision for bees, because they die right after they sting you. The stinger pulls loose from their insides . . . and everyone knows what happens. But it serves them right.

I guess he thought he would have some fun torturing me and landed on my arm. By this time, I'm swerving left, then right, off the road, busting the barbed wire fence, and plowing into the field of sunflowers, mowing them down, and sending cawing blackbirds into terrorized flight.

The bee flitted left and flitted right. I did not want to stop. I wanted the wind to suck the bee out the window. If I stopped, he could land and sting me.

I swerved hard left, crossing the two-lane road, narrowly avoiding an oncoming SUV and a furniture mover semi-truck.

Determined to send the bee elsewhere on its errant flight, I continued cutting the wheel hard right and left, weaving back and forth across the road.

Suddenly, the bee was gone. Relieved, I slowed my car to a stop on the road's shoulder. I looked down at the floorboard, then up at the ceiling. No bee! "Yes!" I shouted, and did a fist pump several times.

Right about then, I noticed the sheriff's vehicle, blue and red lights flashing, parked behind my car. The deputy, a big, muscle-building type, spoke into his loud speaker, "Please place both hands on your steering wheel." In what seemed like eternity, he finally exited his vehicle with a cautious, yet commanding attitude. I could tell by the expression on his face, partially obscured by dark shades, that he considered this event a little more serious than the usual traffic stop.

He stepped up beside my already open window. He did not lean in, but kept one hand firmly on his holstered revolver. "Sir," he stated with a stringent manner that stood in exact opposition to the polite word. "May I see your driver's license and insurance, please?" His teeth gritted.

I fumbled for my license in my wallet. I handed it to him and then dug the insurance card from the glove compartment and handed that to him as well. He pretended to look at them. I am sure he was watching me with at least one eye.

"You see, deputy," I was struggling with just how to explain my behavior as the realization of what I had just done began to sink in. "I'm allergic to bees, and there was a . . ."

He had no intention of listening to my explanation.

In the corner of my eye, I saw a huge, tattooed bulk of a man with a red baseball cap on his head walking quickly towards my car. The cap read, "Yes, I Do Own the Road." His face was as red as the cap.

He hollered, "Is this the jerk that almost got me killed and totally demolished my furniture load?" I could tell immediately that he was the truck driver with whom I narrowly missed colliding.

He pushed past the deputy and stuck a beefy arm in the window. I felt his sweaty, hairy skin brush my face. The deputy would have none of that. He deftly hoisted the trucker's arm and pushed him away from my car.

He turned and faced the man. "None of that, sir," he said with menacing calm. "I'm going to have to ask you to step away from the vehicle."

He dropped his hand to his nightstick on his belt and, with one smooth motion, swung it up, pounding the end in his other palm. My license and insurance form flew from his hand, and the breeze sent them sailing down the road.

I felt relief and panic at the same time. Relief that the intimidating deputy was ready to defend me, and panicked that that tiny bug had thrown my world into chaos. The deputy pointed his nightstick at the trucker. "Back away, sir. Back away."

The trucker was stubborn. He held his ground, hands on his hips. He feinted twice towards the window. The deputy stepped sideways and interceded. He began to say to the trucker, "If you don't back away, sir . . ." when the bee reappeared right at my nose level.

Terror again seized me. Without thinking, I sought escape. I pushed my door open violently. In doing so, I slammed the unsuspecting deputy in the back, knocking him to the ground.

I scrambled out of the car, running in circles, jumping and flinging my arms around like chimpanzees do in the old Tarzan movies. I caught site of the trucker. His eyes were wide, and he was backing away warily. I'm guessing he thought I was on some sort of hallucinogenic drug or escaped from a mental institution.

The deputy was on his feet in no time, stout heart that he was, defender of my life and due comrade, and he duly knocked me down face first to the pavement. He knelt on my back flattening my face and arms against the hot asphalt.

"Ooh, ouch! It's hot!" I shouted, struggling. For such a pretty day, the pavement was burning hot. I began kicking my legs in a vain effort to break free from the heat.

"Lie still!" the deputy shouted.

He grabbed my left arm. He cuffed it. I waved my right arm about, eluding his grasp. "No, I don't want to be arrested!"

The trucker came up. He kicked my legs. He kicked my rear end.

"Step away, sir," the deputy said.

Later I would feel a little sorry for the deputy's predicament. But only a little.

At length, he attained my free arm and cuffed it to the left one and dragged me to my feet up against the side of my car.

He spoke into his shoulder mic. "122 here. Request assistance, county road 114 by the Miller farm." There was some crackling language in response. I couldn't believe it. Me, a man who wouldn't hurt a fly . . . maybe I'd hurt a bee, but for me, the deputy needs *backup*.

With his free hand, he checked my pockets and the outside of my pants legs. Then he swung me around and checked the inside of my pants. I have always wondered why they check the inside of the pants' legs. I've never seen pants with pockets on the inside of the legs.

He spun me around and slammed my back against the car.

"But, sir," I tried to explain, "There was a bee." He was not listening.

Just then, the trucker who had been circling looking for just the right moment saw his opportunity and swept in for a swift kick to my groin. He erred in his trajectory, however, and his leg flew up catching the deputy square in the ribs. The deputy did not flinch. Time stood still as the trucker backed away in slow motion, his attitude an apologetic one. The deputy turned his eyes in a tightly controlled way, slow and steady, and gave the trucker such a look. It was a look like that guy in the movies that says, "I'll be back."

The trucker continued to back up just as another deputy's car pulled up. That deputy exited. "What you need, Clint?" he said. Of course, my deputy was named Clint.

Clint bent over, retrieved his hat and sunglasses from the pavement and donned both.

I was mumbling, "A bee, a bee, a bee."

"Stop your stuttering, son." Clint grabbed hold of my wimpy shoulder with a grip like a vise. "Clark!" he shouted back to the other deputy, "I'm takin' this one in. Reckless driving, resisting arrest, and I'll think of some others. You arrest that guy." He pointed at the trucker.

"What for?" said Clark.

"Assaulting an officer."

"It was a bee, a bee, a bee," I kept saying.

Deputy Clint shoved me in the back of his patrol car.

"Now, you best lie down," he snarled. "I'm going to get you back to the jail fast."

"A bee, a bee . . ." I continued.

"You can tell it to the judge. And you can call your Aunt Bea when we get there." He was seriously not listening to me. He slid into the driver's seat and burned rubber racing me to the jail. He told me my rights. "You have the right to remain silent . . ."

I didn't hear it all, because I was rolling around so hard in the back seat.

When we arrived at the sheriff's office, I never gave up trying to tell everyone I could that it was a bee's fault, but no one there listened either.

They put me in a cell with two bunks that were attached to a brick wall. The cell maintained one nicely cleaned toilet, a sink and a copy of the daily newspaper. A barred window high in the wall had a little yellow, flowered valance across the top. All the comforts of home.

I sat on one of the beds, my head in my hands. A short, rotund female guard with a sweet face walked up. "Did you ever get a hold of your Aunt Bea?" she said.

I shook my head, too weary to explain.

"Well, let me know if you need anything." Her voice had a lilting, sing-song tone.

"Wow," I said to myself. "Room service."

After about an hour of feeling sorry for myself, I rose to look at the newspaper. The headline screamed, "County Cracks Down on Reckless Drivers." Swell. I arrived at just the right time.

I wandered aimlessly to the high barred window. I stood on my tiptoes. I saw a blue, cloudless sky, a jet stream, and . . . in one corner of the building's overhang, a huge hive, writhing with bees.

I stepped back. "Whew," I said, "at least, they're outside." Then I took notice of the number of dead bee bodies lying about the window sill and on the floor. And to my amazement, through a crack in the wooden frame of the window, a bee crawled, flitted a little, then landed on top of the sill.

Before my panic reached fever pitch, I heard the clang of the cell door behind me.

The sweet rotund female guard said, "Looks like you get some company."

In walked the trucker. The guard departed. While I backed away, the trucker's sour look turned to a menacing grin. He began pounding his fist into his hand.

I think he figured he was already in jail, so he didn't care if he got one more assault charge filed against him. His bulk loomed over me. I sank back against the wall. "I'm sorry," I said, "I didn't mean to."

He hovered over me. I could smell his rank body odor and onion breath. I could feel his body tensing to pummel me into a pulp fine enough to make papier mache.

With my eyes closed, in desperation, I gave one last plea. "It wasn't my fault, it was . . ."

"A bee! A bee!" he shouted. He began running around the cell, jumping and waving his arms like those chimpanzees in movies. "I'm allergic to bees!" he cried.

I opened my eyes enough to see the trucker climb on top of a bunk like he was afraid of a mouse. I felt his pain. I knew his fear. I also knew that the bee could at any time come after me. I rose stealthily to my feet. The trucker looked at me with pleading eyes. "I don't want to die," he moaned. "I don't have my epinephrine. Aah, aah, go away." He swatted continuously.

The bee had landed on the trucker's arm. He froze, his eyes wide. I seized upon an idea. Ever so slowly I inched forward. I gathered up the newspaper, folded it twice, good and tight. With all my force, I brought the newspaper club down on the bee. The bee tumbled, flattened, to the floor.

The trucker looked at me with amazement. "You saved my life."

What could I say? I nodded.

"Okay, dude. Friends now?" He extended his hand to me. I shook it, and pounded the rolled paper like a nightstick against my leg, and gave him a look similar to Clint's.

"Alright, dude," the trucker said. "How can I repay you?"

It didn't take much thought. "You can tell the guard that you know it was a bee that attacked me and caused me to drive recklessly."

He paused a moment with an incredulous look. Then he shrugged his shoulders. "Ok. Guard!" he called, "Guard!"

The sweet lady guard entered the hall. "Something I can do for you, honey?"

"Yes," said the trucker with intensity, "I'm willing to fill out an affidavit that the only reason this man drove recklessly was to avoid being stung by a lethal bee."

Right at this moment, Clint strode up. He nodded at the guard and said, "I heard what you said." To me, he said, "Looks like it's your lucky day, you little wimp. Mr. Miller is *not* going to file charges for you tearing up his fence and his field of sunflowers. He said the insurance company offered him twice what the crop was worth. And if this guy will fill out that affidavit, looks like you're free to go."

With my eyes wide in amazement, the guard opened the cell door, escorted me back to the front to get my things, helped me sign out, and told the clerk to drop the charges. I was free to go. The trucker, named Bob, sends me emails whenever he's at home, and I return a message to him. We've become quite close.

NIGHTMARE

Larry Morris

*D*ON'T FALL ASLEEP. Or is it *don't wake up?*

It's raining again, and that doesn't make it any easier to stay awake. I haven't slept for, I can't remember, maybe two days. I can't ever sleep again. I must not. It will come back. I know it will.

I remember when I was growing up, my family would visit my elderly aunt who lived alone way back in the woods in the middle of nowhere. My father would grow angrier with every pothole we hit on the way. It seemed like it rained every time I took a nap there. Funny how you remember things like that. The rain still makes me sleepy.

I haven't left the bedroom since I woke up the last time. I'm afraid I'll find that nothing really happened at all. Getting hungry too. All I've had to eat were those crackers I brought in with me before I fell asleep. I finally got the nerve to peek out of the bedroom window and look outside. Pulling the curtains back just an inch or two, I looked at the front lawn.

It's gone! There's not even a trace of where it had been. It had gotten past the big rosebush last time. It keeps getting closer each time I fall asleep. I can't sleep! Green, straight grass. Long. I haven't done much of anything with the house since this started. No time for that. I looked closer. Not even an impression where it had crawled. No blood either. I know I hit it last time. I can still hear its scream.

The Nelson boy was riding by on his bike with the morning paper. He flung it hard, and as it hit the stoop, I noticed three others lying there undisturbed. Out by the curb, the neighborhood cars were parked where they always were in the morning. No spaceship. Not even a burn mark on the street where it had landed. The rain had stopped, and the sun was trying to come out. People were starting to move about and do whatever it was they did with their daily lives. Old man Cramer was up and out on the stoop to get his paper already. Nothing strange. The same old neighborhood.

I closed the curtains and crossed the bedroom to the door that opens onto the hallway. Hunger had finally won out. My hand was shaking so badly I could hardly hold the doorknob. Sweat trickled down my back as I turned the knob and opened the door just a crack. I could hear the air conditioner running in the living room. That meant it was a hot, sticky day already. The grandfather clock was ticking. It sounded like it was in one piece. The refrigerator just kicked on. Nothing else. It sounded just like my house should sound. I opened the door wide and stepped out into the hallway.

The light over the medicine cabinet in the guest bathroom was on, but then it always was. The living room was dark with the curtains drawn. The morning sun was shining through the kitchen window into the other end of the hallway.

I went down the hall and edged into the living room staying close to the wall. Just as I got past the opening into the room, the grandfather clock at my elbow chimed and I almost jumped out of my skin. Seven times it chimed. Still early. And the clock was, indeed, undisturbed. Upright, and against the wall where I had put it the day I brought it home from my aunt's. It had sounded so real when it toppled over and hit the other side of the hallway. I looked around at the spot where I had heard it hit. No hole, not even a mark on the wall.

I had to calm down. Nothing had happened. It was just a dream. This was my house in my neighborhood and nothing was wrong. Everything was normal. Wasn't it?

As my eyes adjusted to the semi-darkness of the living room, I could see everything was just as I had left it the day before yesterday.

My coat was on the chair by the door where I had left it. The door!! Was it locked? I ran over, almost tripping over the foot stool in front of the easy chair, and grabbed at the lock. Still bolted. Just like before.

I looked around at the rest of the room. The rocking chair by the fireplace was upright. The lamp on the table beside it was in one piece and not shattered on the floor. It hadn't really happened at all. Then another thought struck me.

I ran across the room into the den and snapped on the light. The gun cabinet next to the window was still locked, all the guns in place. At the window, I pulled the curtain aside and saw the glass intact and, below it, clean carpet. No shell casings. Just a dream. But it had come back again and again and it kept getting closer each time. I had heard it scream, hadn't I?

I was so tired. Maybe the food would help after all. I was hungry enough. I drug myself into the kitchen. The bright, morning sun streamed in through the window over the sink, reflecting off of dirty dishes everywhere. But none of them were broken. See, I told you; I said to myself; it is just a silly dream. The dishes were stacked up in the sink and on the kitchen table in the process of growing something from the dried, crusted food that was now days old. But none of them were broken.

I made myself a sandwich from the last of the bread and luncheon meat and took it back into the living room. As I sat in the dark and wolfed down the food, I kept an eye on the front door, just to make sure. Even though it was a dream. Wasn't it? It had sounded so close to the front door the last time. I have to think of something. Something to stop it.

The phone rang, and I was so startled I dropped the plate. I looked at my hands and they were shaking. It took four rings before I thought I had calmed down enough to answer it. It was work calling to see how my flu was doing. I lied again and told them it was getting worse. Yes, I had called a doctor about it and yes; I was taking my medicine. It was just going to take some time. They reminded me again about the doctor's note I'd need when I got back. I thanked them and hung up, wondering darkly if they would accept a note from the coroner. Just a dream, I thought. With what little of the sandwich I had managed to eat and the phone call, I felt a little more awake.

I went back into my bedroom and crossed over to the master bath. My reflection in the mirror over the sink looked almost like a stranger. My hair was going in all directions and a three day growth of beard made me look like one of the guys you tripped over in some of the more interesting sections of town. And my eyes were a mass of red, completely bloodshot, worse than I had ever seen them. A quick shower at least made me feel close to human. I shaved and brushed my teeth and then looked back into the mirror at my face. The only thing I couldn't fix was my eyes. The fatigue still showed.

As I walked back into the living room pulling on a clean shirt, I noticed the odor. It must be the kitchen. Three days of leftover food and dirty dishes. As I moved to the kitchen it got stronger. I hadn't noticed it before the shower because I probably smelled worse. I chanced opening the back door just a crack to let in some fresh air. It smelled so good. Still thick and heavy even after the morning sprinkle, but good.

I thought of the thing in the front yard and the fatigue came back. But, it's just a dream. Nothing really happened. The fresh air felt so good. I opened the back-door wide and looked outside. The same old, neglected grass as out front. And the garage. I held onto the kitchen counter to keep from weaving. Getting sleepier.

Then it hit me. In the garage, I had something that would stop it. I pushed open the screen door and stumbled out into the back yard. Way in the back of the big two car structure, under the painting tarps was the old chest from my military days. I had no idea where the key was anymore, so I grabbed a hammer off of the workbench and madly swung at the heavy lock. The third blow snapped it off. After rummaging like a crazy man through the chest and throwing things over my shoulder for what seemed like an eternity, I found it. An old pineapple-shaped hand grenade. A relic from the past I was not supposed to have.

How stupid, I thought as my shoulders slumped. I slowly starting crying as I realized what I was doing. This was taking over my sanity.

It was only a crazy dream. You can't blow up a dream. I had to stop this. And I had to sleep.

I got to my feet still holding the rusted relic and staggered back into the house. I left the back door open to let the kitchen air out and moved back into the living room. Tossing the grenade onto the couch, I slumped into the easy chair. I had no choice; the fatigue took over as I closed my eyes and thought about all the things I must do. The people at work would only play this game so long. And then I thought about the thing on the front lawn. Then I cried. And cried. And slept.

*   *   *

I was standing in my bedroom listening to the clock strike one, two, three times. No light coming from the bedroom window so it must be three in the morning. I looked out the window. Dark and quiet. Three in the morning and no cars out front? The dream. It's back! I felt wide awake. Looking out the bedroom door I could see the darkened hallway. As I slowly walked towards the door, the rumbling came.

Just like all the other times it started low and far off. All the other times? Can you remember a dream from a dream? Then it got louder and louder. It sounded like the inside of an earthquake. I covered my ears and fell to the floor screaming. The rumbling turned into a piercing shriek so loud that I thought I would pass out. Then it landed.

The house shook like it had been hit with a wrecking ball. Dishes smashed to the floor in the kitchen and I could hear them shatter into the hallway. The grandfather clock tipped and sounded like it had knocked a hole into the opposite wall. Things were flying all around me. Books, pieces of furniture, clothes. I could hear wood splintering in the living room and it sounded like windows breaking somewhere. Maybe in the den. Then everything was quiet. The lights had gone out.

I got up off the floor and dusted myself off. I was moving so slowly. What was wrong, I wasn't tired? It took a few minutes for my eyes to adjust to the darkness. The bedroom was in shambles. The mirror on the vanity was cracked, and the bed was standing on only two legs.

It seemed like it took hours for me to turn around and walk to the hallway. Like being in a swimming pool. That was it! Like I was standing in something waist-deep. Something liquid. I just couldn't seem to move.

Just like all the other times, the grandfather clock had tipped over and wedged itself against the opposite wall almost blocking the entrance to the living room. I could just barely see it in the darkness. As I moved toward it I slowed down even more.

I couldn't get over the clock. I never could. All arms and legs, I felt so heavy and slow. And the clock kept moving. Just as I would reach up to hold onto the top of it, it would move 2 or 3 inches to the left or right. I always moved so slow and it wouldn't hold still. Then I would finally remember I couldn't climb over it and I would crawl under it into the living room.

The living room was a mess as always. Fragments of the antique lamp all over the floor next to the overturned rocker. The easy chair on its side and ashes from the fireplace all over the room. I was looking over the horribly familiar scene when I heard the rustling out front on the lawn.

I knew what it was and I couldn't move. It sounded like someone was dragging something across the lawn. Something heavy. It would stop for a few seconds and then start up again. Closer. Much closer than the last time.

I could move much faster now. It always happened this way. I went into the den very quietly and stood next to the window. I know what I would see next. I ducked low and went to the other side of the window. Mustn't let it see me. I pulled the curtain back just a few inches and looked outside.

The spaceship was back. It loomed huge over the street lights with steam and smoke rolling out from underneath. The pavement had buckled under its weight. The large door in the center of the front had been rolled open and left that way and there was a trail of smoking, bubbling slime running up to the end of the sidewalk.

Just like before. Except for one thing. I strained my eyes to look closer. It was old man Cramer. Or at least what was left of him. Everything from the waist down was buried beneath the spaceship.

The morning paper was still in his hand. But this is the dream. He's not supposed to be in it. He's lying right where he had been this morning. This morning?

I ran back into the living room feeling less and less sure about where I was. Most things were like they had been the other times, but then there were things that weren't.

The noise outside stopped me in front of the picture window by the easy chair. Scratching. It was scratching on the cement stoop. God, that's close! It can't be! It's only been a few minutes. How long had it been? I looked through the curtains by the easy chair and just as I did, a two-foot, scaly claw came through the window and caught me just above the jaw. I flew back and hit the wall beside the fireplace. The whole side of my face was on fire. As I rolled over and touched my face with my hand, I saw the slimy claw trying to break the other window panes. The front door looked like it was being hit by a battering ram. It was trying to get in at the window and the door.

As I got up, I felt the blood run down my face. Wait, on the couch! The grenade! I turned and looked. It was there! But, this was the dream. I picked it up and pulled the pin. I looked back to the window, and the claw was gone. Confused, I threw the relic through the window and fell down beside the couch.

The blast ripped the front door off its hinges and blew it back into the living room along with what seemed like half of the front yard. Dust and dirt flew everywhere. The living room looked like a battle field. I slowly edged my way toward the front doorway in the smoke and looked outside. Just as I looked around the door jamb, it sprang.

*   *   *

I jumped as the clock in the hallway chimed. I was still sitting in the easy chair in the living room drenched with sweat. The dream, it had come again. I scrambled out of the chair and crouched in the middle of the floor. Nothing changed. Damn! The window good as new. No hole where the door had been. Just the door. I spun around. I could just make out in the dark the rusted relic of the past lying on the couch where I had tossed it earlier that morning.

Too weary to care, I got up and went to the front door and threw it open. It was night. A cool night, a quiet neighborhood; no monster. I closed the door not noticing the deep slash that ran corner to corner about an inch deep. Almost all the way through. It was probably for the best.

I turned and walked down the hallway toward the kitchen. I didn't remember until it was too late that I had left the door open to the back yard. No one heard me scream as I was dragged off to the spaceship still smoking beside the garage. The creature pulled me inside and the spaceship took off.

* * *

The attendant looked through the window as he passed the locked door and noticed that the new patient was in the fetal position in the corner.

"Hank," he yelled over his shoulder. "Get the doctor. The new guy has had another episode."

Why I Wrote This Story

I have always loved the old Twilight Zone TV show and, later, Rod Serling's most bizarre show, Night Gallery. They both brought to us strange stories we would have never thought of and, more to the point, stories that usually had a twist at the end no one ever saw coming. These have always been my favorite types of horror and suspense stories and I couldn't resist trying one.

"WHO'S TRUMAN?"

Dick Elam

DIM LIGHT INSIDE the bottom of the Japanese merchant ship helped.

The fire heated the rivets, but gave off little light. Kept the guards from watching how they filled the rivet holes. Also, thank goodness, the fire also furnished welcomed warmth.

Lee knew their guards hadn't caught on. The Japanese hadn't figured out that Lee and Gregg inserted mud to fill the rivet hole they had drilled to connect the ship's pieces of iron. The mud stuffing would make the rivet look flush.

The inspector wouldn't notice the *Melicans* had slipped a smaller size rivet into the connecting hole. But when the merchant ship went to sea, salt water would wash away the mud, and the rivet hole would leak. Lee hoped he would live long enough to hear their sabotage worked.

The two prisoners raised their hand and waved.

The Japanese guard understood that meant the *Melicans* needed more rivets. The guard nodded, took the empty box with him, and climbed the ladder.

Lee sat, leaned against the interior hull. "God, I wish we were taking a smoke break. You know, Gregg, I can count—on one hand—every cigarette I've smoked since 'Dugout Doug' left on his submarine."

"Lee, You really don't like MacArthur, do you?"

"It's personal, Gregg."

"Got that. But, remember President Roosevelt ordered Mac to leave Corregidor by submarine."

"I bought that. President still Commander-in-Chief, and my family voted for FDR, but if we . . ."

"Work! Work!" Their guard was climbing back down the ladder, the bag of rivets across his shoulder.

"No talk! No talk"! the fat guard yelled.

Ichazumi always sounded authoritative with what little English vocabulary he had developed. "No food. No talk. March. No lights. No slow . . . go fast." And lately, Itchy had learned some American city names:

"We bomb you, Nu York. We bomb you, *Wasz-in-ton*."

The guard handed them the bag of rivets. With his other hand, Itchy held the wooden cudgel. The implement looked like a baseball bat, but Lee knew Itchy brandished a lethal weapon. Another Corregidor captive didn't survive the blow. Lee had been ordered to help bury Marvin four days ago.

Two young, maybe 17-year-old, Japanese soldiers looked down to watch the workers inside the hull. Strapped over their shoulders, they carried World War One rifles. Their frozen faces suggested they didn't understand, or care, what Itchy was trying to say in his pidgin English. They looked, and were, unneeded. Lee knew that for every American POW who tried to escape, the Japanese were known to kill two inmates.

And escape to where? Swim across the bay to Tokyo?

If Tokyo Rose's radio sweet talk had any truth to it, you would have to keep swimming to Hawaii to escape. And she reminded, often, that Pearl Harbor was still a cemetery. Didn't she understand her slurs only stiffened resistance?

In addition to Rose's propaganda, their guard also furnished daily war reports.

A week ago, Itchy had chanted military claims: " We bomb bat-ships. We bomb *Mack-ar-tur*."

Earlier that week, Lee and Gregg had been bussed to their annual Red Cross medical checkup, per Geneva Convention rules. As the bus crept forward, they could see some Japanese men wearing yellow sashes pulling debris off the street.

"We bomb Yok-o-hama", Lee thought.

They sat at the back of the bus where they could talk.

Gregg whispered, "Lee, I've listened to you for five years. I think Rose told us more than Itchy intended when she joked about MacArthur returning to the Philippines.

You still don't like the man. What's really bothering you about MacArthur?"

Lee waited until Itchy started a conversation with the bus driver. Then he replied.

"Two days before Dugout-Doug left Corregidor, I met him in a tunnel. I had been three days sitting, sometimes sleeping, sometimes firing at Jap planes from our machine-gun emplacement outside a tunnel . . ."

Lee rubbed his face when he saw the guard look back. When Itchy turned and looked forward, Lee resumed whispering behind his open hand.

"My jaw was swollen. I had a tooth killing me. My buddies finally called another Marine to come up out of the tunnel replace me. They insisted I go to the infirmary . . ."

Itchy looked back, and Lee coughed loudly into his hand. The guard said something in Japanese. Lee guessed Itchy didn't know how to say, "No cough!" But Lee gave his head a deferential bow, which seemed to satisfy the guard.

When Itchy looked forward, Lee continued. "Inside the tunnel, going to sick bay, I met the General.

"I saluted. And MacArthur barked, 'Soldier, you need a shave, and change your uniform.' And he walked on. Good thing I didn't know, or I would have asked him if he was hurrying to catch his submarine? And, probably, I would have got court-martialed."

Gregg had chuckled, then, but now Itchy waved his wooden club toward the ladder. The two prisoners hurried to climb. At the top of the ladder, Lee felt the chilling wind. Little daylight remained, but enough light to see smoke still rose from Tokyo across the bay. Last night they had heard the sirens announcing the air raid. While they shivered on their cots, they had heard bombs explode.

When Itchy marched the prisoners to breakfast, Lee estimated he saw, at least, a dozen different Tokyo fires. Now, Itchy assembled his prisoners of war on the dock, waved his club, pointed to their barracks.

Lee and Gregg swung their arms to their sides, marched. They had learned to survive by restraining any show of emotion.

They lowered their heads—but kept their shoulders raised—as they walked the dock. Their eyes moved to scan the Yokohama harbor. Blackened damage appeared everywhere. Some fires still ate at nearby buildings—except for the bamboo huts that comprised the POW quarters.

Two days ago, the only day in the year when American POWs were bussed to the Red Cross Building for medical checkups, B-29s had bombed the shipyard where they slaved everyday. Forget the Jap's propaganda, Lee thought. Washington bombed, not likely when we're bombing Yokohama.

Two more prisoners climbed out of the freighter hull, and fell in line. The Americans marched, by twos, inside the fence, marched on to the dining area. Even the waiting wilted rice dinner didn't cause the men to slouch.

Itchy allowed them enough time to visit the latrine, before he aimed his cudgel, pointed to the dining area.

Makoto, the one-eyed cook, often taunted prisoners who passed his food table. When Allied bombs started falling across the bay, he had greeted each prisoner with a scowl and sarcastic words from his limited English category. This evening Makoto smiled.

Unlike Itchy, Makoto knew enough English to make fun of the prisoners. Enough English to serve a small amount of banter as the men passed in the chow-line.

Yesterday, Makoto didn't smile when Gregg snapped back. "Our compound wasn't bombed. Your shipyard was." Makoto frowned, but he wasn't supposed to speak to prisoners. He didn't call for Itchy to hit Gregg.

Today, Makoto beamed. He knew something we didn't.

The cook looked both ways, to make sure Japanese guards weren't looking, before Makoto whispered a message as he served. Lee could see Makoto's words whispered from one member of the chow line back to another. Then Jones in front of Lee passed on the message:

"FDR died . . . Harry Truman your President now."

At first opportunity, Lee passed back the news to Gregg.

Gregg's face clouded. When the Guard wasn't looking, Gregg whispered back the news and asked::

"Who's Harry Truman?"

Lee rolled his eyes right, left, shook his head. Shrugged his shoulders. The line moved forward, and Lee held out his plate to receive Makoto's three spoons of rice and something that looked like cabbage.

At the table, the men filled their cups, passed the water jug from one end to the other. Lee drank three cups of water. Water helped fill his stomach.

When—Lee didn't want to think 'if'—they were free, he vowed to drink three beers a meal. His older fishing buddy back home on the Yellow River worked at the hospital. He had told Lee that beer was the perfect food. 'Metabolizes well'. Lee wasn't sure what his older buddy was telling him. But he would look up the word in the family dictionary if he got home.

Home. Back home in Indiana. He had only been back there twice after he graduated from high school and joined the Marines, back when Franklin Roosevelt was nominated to run for a third term.

And, now, he worried that Makoto spoke true. The cook even added a new name. "True-man. Harry True-man." Sounded more like a promise than a family name.

Lee wondered if Itchy had been half-right. That the Japanese had bombed Washington. That FDR was not only dead, but so was the vice-president, and maybe the new President had been the Speaker from Congress.

As they were marched to their barrack. Lee whispered to the prisoner behind him. "Pete, you know who's Harry Trueman?"

Pete whispered back. "I'm from Missouri. We had a local politician by that name. Member of the Prendergast machine. The machine took good care of my family. Had a politician named Truman. Haberdasher, who went broke . . ."

Itchy heard someone talking. Yelled at our marching line. "No talk! No Talk!"

Pete waited until Itchy turned his head. Then whispered, "No way Harry Truman is President of the United States."

Sirens sounded.

Lee smiled, thought. Our bombers are headed this way again. Sent by command from Washington, D.C. Thank you, Mr. President. I may get back home before I die.

Harry--whatever name our new President Harry Truman answers to--give 'em hell, Harry.

* * *

Why I Wrote This Story

Historical fiction rests on some truth. In 1955, as we drove from Abilene to Shreveport, trailing our sailboat, Lee Finch told me about Corregidor and the Yokohama prisoner-of war camp. I've embroidered his story with invented dialogue and added some research findings.

Lee died in Texas, but he lives in the first and last chapters of the World War II historical novel I am now writing. ###

TEXAS TWO-STEP

George W Ramphrey

Chapter I

MY BIRTH NAME was Robert "Bob" Randall, seventy-two years old, and resided in Mesquite, Texas most of my life. The Buckner Children's Home in Dallas was my home until I was eighteen. I was clueless as to who my parents were or where they lived for that matter. I had no regrets of my childhood because the Home was an excellent educational facility. There was an outstanding faculty, and lifelong friendships developed. They taught me the value of working hard. The campus was self-sufficient, and we raised crops, livestock, and a little hell at times. I recently retired as a mechanic and my last employment was at Joe's Garage and Repair Shop off Highway 175 in Seagoville. I was tickled-pink when the garage employees and management, presented me a Timex watch, service plaque, and a steak dinner for two at Hungry Cowboys Diner on Elam Road. I played guitar as a part-time musician for over fifty-years. I prided myself because I played a Merle Travis picking fingerstyle. Only a few guitar players mastered his playing technique. My band "Bucking Bob and the Skeeter Cowboy Band" played most weekends at the Tear-Drop Inn in Dallas on Irving Boulevard. We played there as the house band. Occasionally, we booked other gigs in the Dallas area.

My wife, Sadie was the love of my life. We met as teenagers when she brought her car in for maintenance when I worked part-time at Lucky's Garage in Forney. I knew from the moment that I saw her that she would be my wife. I never dated or had eyes for any other woman. Petite with red hair and green eyes, she had the prettiest milky skin you've ever seen. Even with her pigeon-toed malady, I thought that she was perfect. She was a church-going woman who kept me on the straight and narrow. I was never a grand prize at five-feet eight inches tall and two-hundred and twenty pounds. The boys at the garage said that I was uglier than a muddy fence. My red bulbous nose resembled an overripe Vidalia onion. However, Sadie told me that a big nose doesn't mess up an attractive face. She loved me in spite of my shortcomings. We had two children, and they lived out of state. Our oldest, Kitty, had red-hair like her mother and was happily married with twins Mandy and Sandy. She resided in Topeka, Kansas with husband Jake, the manager of Sonny's Used Car Lot. Our son Eddie was intelligent and handsome and lived in New Orleans. He owned and operated an Antique Store in the French Quarter off Bourbon Street. Even though in his forties, he remained single. He told me that he was married to his job. I was always proud of my children. The way I looked at it as long as they were happy then that's what matters. Everyone needed to live their own lives the way they saw appropriate. Life was too short. I taught them not to judge or be judged and don't let people make decisions for you. I thought that growing up in an orphanage, gave me a different perspective on what's important in life.

Ever since I approached seventy years of age, I noticed that many of my lifelong friends had physically and mentally gone downhill. The Good Lord was good to me, and I thought that it was time to start giving back. I felt as spry and physically able as a thirty-five-year-old man. Whoever my parents were; they left me with good genes. Lately, I practiced guitar and worked-up a short list of songs. I volunteered at Pleasant Grove Senior Home Facility to play a free concert to honor my friends. I thought that it was good that they heard old songs again. Hopefully, the pleasant memories were just what the doctor ordered. My band broke up several years ago when drummer and best friend Leo passed away. The other band members went on with their lives. They were either too old or disinterested in playing a gig.

Anyway, I wanted to play the gig solo! For weeks I brushed-up on old songs and added a few new numbers to my repertoire. The majority of my song list was from songs by Hank Williams, Bob Wills and the Texas Playboys, Lefty Frizzell, Jim Reeves, Sons of the Pioneers, Light Crust Doughboys, and Hank Thompson and the Brazos River Valley Boys. It was the social gala event of the year, and I couldn't wait!

"Bob! Turn that infernal music down; you're about to drive me crazy with all that noise."

"Sweetheart, I'm not that loud, am I?"

"I don't think that you realize how much you have that Fender Twin Reverb amp turned up. Please check the volume. My ears are beginning to buzz, and I'm getting a headache."

"The volume is on four."

"Well, turn it down to one or two because I can't hear Pat Sajak on Wheel of Fortune."

"What's Vanna White wearing?"

"She's wearing one of the prettiest floral gowns that I've ever seen. She's one beautiful woman."

"You know what my darling? I think you're prettier than her."

"Bob Randall! Flattery will get you everywhere. In fact, I'm cooking your favorite dish tonight. I'm getting ready to put on a pot of Spaghetti and meatballs, and for dessert, we'll have banana pudding and your favorite beverage, sweet tea."

"Yes indeed, that meal is a Texas State Fair blue-ribbon winner."

"By the way, what was that song that you were playing earlier? You know that fast, zippy two-step. I'm not familiar with that number?"

"That's a song by the new artist George Strait and is entitled '*Big Balls in Cowtown!*' Bob Wills and the Texas Playboys recorded it first. I know that you've heard it performed before. Please don't tell me that you've forgotten that classic."

"Maybe so, but if I did, it's been awhile back for sure. I don't listen to the new stuff on the radio much anymore."

Bob stared at Sadie and noticed her hair was disheveled on her brow and had playfully curled into a unique pattern. Her green eyes shone radiantly with a glow of love. He took a deep sigh and gave her a warm embrace.

"I love you, sweetheart!"

"I love you back big boy, but don't get all sentimental on me." She said as she affectionately rubbed and pinched his stomach through his western cowboy shirt. "What would John Wayne say?"

"The heck with what the Duke thinks! You've been a wonderful wife and mother, and I just wanted to let you know how much I appreciate all your efforts and sacrifices. You've made a good life for the kids and me, and I could've never asked for more."

"Well, you're welcome! You haven't been a slouch yourself. You've always been a great Father and a wonderful Husband."

"Well, before I get all choked-up and dewy-eyed, I'd better put away my guitar and help you cook that spaghetti."

"No sir, you can sit down at the dining room table and talk to me, but if you stick your big nose into my pots, you'll lose it."

"Feisty! I like it!"

"Well, come on and join me in the kitchen, but turn-off that den light when you leave. Do you realize that our bill last month was nearly two-hundred dollars?"

"Highway robbery if you ask me."

"Well, hurry-up Diamond Jim and join me while I cook."

"OK, sugar booger! I'm coming."

They set up their TV trays and enjoyed their meal while watching a rerun of "Dragnet." After Channel 8 news they called it a night.

"Goodnight sweetheart," Sadie said as she slipped into her double-bed.

"Goodnight back at you. I just wanted to tell you that I'm looking forward to playing this gig. I can't believe how many of our friends have bad health."

"I know because God has been good to us. We're both blessed with good health except for your bad back, from years of the heavy lifting when you were a mechanic."

"Well, good night darling and don't let the bedbugs bite."

"Would it be Ok with you if I read awhile? I'm a little restless."

"Go ahead! What are you reading?"

"It's a romantic novel entitled, *"Passionate Lovers in Paris."*

"Is that Paris, Texas or Paris, France?"

"What do you think?"

"Probably the latter, let me see that book for a moment?"

"Who's that man on the cover?"

"That's the model Fabio!"

"My God, that boy must work out! Look at that six-pack!"

"Don't you have a six-pack too?"

"Yes, but my six-pack is under ice."

Sadie laughed out loud at the comment. "Go to sleep, you silly boy. I love you, not Fabio!"

"Well, thank goodness, that you love me in spite of all my shortcomings."

"It's what's inside a person's heart that matters. Please remember that I'll always love you, sweetie."

The night fell, and darkness consumed the town like a voracious animal. The stars twinkled brightly as an occasional shooting star blazed across the evening sky. The moonlight illuminated the countryside as the wind blew softly through the branches of chinaberry and cedar trees in the front yard. The wind chimes, tied to a branch of a red oak tree, jingled like ice clinking in a drinking glass. Except for an occasional lone-barking dog or distant sounds of yelping coyotes, the night was tranquil and peaceful. The train track, within a quarter of a mile from their home, was a noisy aggravation. A train passed in the wee hours and blew its whistle as the ground rumbled. This combination of sounds awakened Bob. He went into the kitchen and drank a glass of milk and ate a bowl of banana pudding. He returned to bed and tried not to awaken Sadie. However, she turned over and said, "What in the world are you doing up at this late hour?"

"It's that dang train passing by tooting that whistle like an excited child at a birthday party." Bob looked at her and was surprised that in the darkness, her appearance was beautiful and youthful. He asked, "Is it OK if I sleep next to you the rest of the night?"

"Will your back be OK?"

"I think so."

"Well, sure, come on in," she said while she pulled back her cover and made room for him with welcoming arms. "Will you do me a favor when you play the gig at Pleasant Grove home?"

"Sure, anything you want. What is it?"

"Please, play my favorite song by Jim Reeves. You know our song."

"Yes, of course, I'll play 'Put Your Sweet Lips' just for you, my love."

After a few minutes, she turned over and exhaled a deep breath and fell into a deep slumber. After Bob kissed her shoulder and rearranged a pillow, he stared at the ceiling for a few minutes. He thought about how lucky he was and how his life was blessed. They were proud parents of two-kids and two-grandchildren. However, his greatest gift was his dear wife. He prayed to God and thanked him for all his blessings. He thought about the gig and then drifted off.

The next morning, he found a note that Sadie had left earlier to buy groceries at Kroger's. He picked up his guitar and plugged in his amp and practiced his set-list. Bob was concerned because, after a couple of hours, Sadie hadn't called or returned. At noon, he nervously jumped-up and answered the phone. He received devastating news.

Chapter II

The following Saturday, he dressed in his best Western shirt and jeans. He wore a pair of full-quill ostrich boots that Sadie had bought him for their fiftieth-wedding anniversary. He cascaded in English Leather cologne and slicked his hair back with Fitch hair oil. He tied a red bandana around his neck and headed out the door with guitar and amp in hand. Bob greeted everyone at the Pleasant Grove facility and met many friends with severe health issues. Nevertheless, he plugged in and played, and the residents of the home were ecstatic. He played the songs like a true professional. His voice was never better, and his rhythm and lead guitar parts were impressive. After he played his favorite Texas two-steps and waltzes, he ended the night by playing the song that he'd promised Sadie. He cleared his throat and with a teardrop, in his voice, he sang, "Put your sweet lips a little closer to the phone, let's pretend that we're together all alone." There wasn't a dry eye in the facility. After the song ended, he carefully placed his guitar into his case. He felt satisfied that he'd made a difference in his friend's lives that night. They hugged him, and everyone shook his hand and patted his back.

The lights were turned on, and he loaded his equipment, full of positive thoughts. On the drive home, he thought of Sadie and whispered, "Sweetheart, I wish you were with me tonight because everything was perfect." He wanted to see her and tell her how well the gig went. Of course, she was asleep, but wouldn't mind if he woke her. He arrived home, and ran into his house and left his guitar and amplifier in the car.

"Sadie! I'm home, sweetheart," he shouted. There wasn't an answer.

"What's going on? Sadie, where are you?" He desperately searched every room. He was upset and confused because she wasn't home. He sank into his recliner, in the living room, and tried to remember if she'd told him where she was going. Was she visiting our children? Where could she be? He thought as he stared-out the front window of the empty house while tears streamed down his face.

At the Pleasant Grove Senior Home, two adults entered for a visit. They signed the visitor's sheet and went to the nurse's station.

An attractive nurse with raven eyes and black hair said, "I'm so glad to meet you, my name is Nurse Jennifer Ralston."

"Nice to meet you too, I'm Kitty, and this is my brother Eddie, and our father Bob Randall is a patient here."

"I've traveled from New Orleans, and my sister came from Kansas to see our father," Eddie said.

"Well, I want to thank you both for coming such a long distance on such a small notice, to see about your father."

"You're welcome, but what's the problem with Daddy?"

"Well, his prognosis is bad, he's critically ill because of massive strokes."

"Will he be able to respond at all? Will he know us?"

"No, he hasn't been able to communicate with anyone in years.

However, lately, he's been working his fingers back and forth and smiling like he's reminiscing about someone or something. He lives in his private world. I've been his nurse for the past year. He doesn't receive many visitors."

"We feel horrible and guilty, but we live so far away, and with a combination of job and family responsibilities, we don't get many chances to visit. In fact, we haven't been home since Mother's funeral a year ago."

"How did you lose your mother?"

"She died in a car wreck last year, and Daddy never recovered. He was devoted to her and lost the will to live. After she passed away, he had a massive stroke, and we admitted him to this facility."

"Well, let's go to his room and visit him."

They entered his room, and observed a lonely figure, in a wheelchair, staring out the window. They hugged and kissed him, but he didn't respond.

A few minutes later, Kitty said, "I believe that he's trying to say something," She bent over and positioned her ear next to his lips and listened. He uttered soft sounds as he moved his fingers.

"What did he say?"

He said, "Let's pretend we're together all alone."

Kitty said with tears in her eyes, "Daddy, you're not alone. I'm your daughter Kitty, and that's your son Eddie. We've come to see you. We both love you, Daddy."

Bob was in a catatonic state, and there wasn't a response. He stared-out the window.

After about ten minutes, Nurse Ralston said, "Well, I better go, will you be here long?"

"No, we're leaving tomorrow. Nurse, we'll walk you out because there's no need to visit anymore since he doesn't know us or realize what's going on. We're staying at the Ramada Inn tonight, and we'll try and visit in the morning on our way out." They kissed him on the forehead and exited the room.

Later, the night nurse came in, she showered, fed, and put him to bed.

About midnight, Bob was awakened by a bright image. He sat up on his bed and said, "Sadie is that you sweetheart?"

"Yes, my darling it's me, I've never left you."

She softly touched his face and gazed into his eyes.

"My darling, I've been lost and missed you so much. Please never leave me again."

"Nothing will ever separate us again. We'll be together forever. The time has come for you to go away with me."

As they lovingly embraced, Bob closed his eyes.

Why I Wrote This Story

Texas Two-Step was inspired by a friend who I admired. He had a great attitude, lived a simple life, loved his wife and family, and was a gifted Texas-Swing musician. He was a blue collar worker who supplemented his income with weekend gigs. He was happy with his life until he lost a loved one. Then, he questioned his existence and struggled with the meaning of life itself. Because he was an eternal optimist, I concluded the story on a positive tone. I wanted to remember him as the happy person he was before tragedy derailed his life.

THE LESSON

Joseph Willis

THE STADIUM WAS quiet. A bird chirped in the background. Sixth thousand people sat, waiting for the event to start. Millions more watched at home. Finally, a microphone popped. The crowd came alive. A single man strode to the center of stage.

The microphone looked small in his hands. He paused as four gigantic screens were lowered. He raised the mike to his lips and he spoke.

"Ladies and Gentlemen, Welcome to the Super Debate," He paused as the crowd roared its approval. "After two months of intense competition, these two teams stand ready to contest for the greatest prize in the land, Super Debate Champion! These teams have come through the competition undefeated, ready to challenge the other team for dominance."

"The format is simple. Each speaker will speak twice with a constructive speech, a cross examination, and later a rebuttal speech." The President of the US and the other elites sat on the field around the contestants.

As the four debater's face was flashed across the screen, a huge crowd of young women, screaming, sprang loose from the police barrier, knocking down the chairs as they raced on stage to touch these handsome gladiators. Security raced to interrupt the surging crowd but some of the girls got through. Once order was re-established, the judges signaled the contestants to start.

*   *   *

Jacob stared at the video, his jaw slack as he watched the "Super Debate" broadcast. He yelled at the broadcast, "I am so tired of hearing about these guys. You can not escape them. They are on every billboard in the damn place. Every screen is filled with these guys selling everything from deodorant to used cars. I hate these bastards." He flung his drink at the screen, shattering the glass. "They are all over the internet." Everyone is talking about this damn debate.

The world bowed down to their skill and intellect. Countless hours of TV time and social media time was spent in worship. Yeah, they are smart and clever. They make great arguments and used words that he did not understand at all. Damn them!

He was in deep trouble. Sent home from school again for not doing his homework was a joke. Stupid rules! Dad was still mad. Jacob glanced across the room. Dad glared back.

"Why can't you be skilled like these people? Look at that clever idea! You could do that."

"Dad!"

Father ignored him. "It is terrible. You didn't even make the JV. All those remedial logic schools, you failed? Don't you care about your future? You think I am made of money?"

"Sorry Dad but I have never been good at debating."

"First true thing you've said." His father slammed the door behind him.

Jacob sank lower in his chair. He flipped the TV off. Dad hates me. Bottom ten percent of the class. Life sucks.

The debate over, the four contestants waited for the decision. They waved to the crowd, texting and posing as the judges considered their fate. The debate master spoke.

"We have a decision." The crowd fell silent, expecting their team to win. "On a four to three decision, the Super Debate

Champion is the LA Marauders Team of Jones/Padilla." The crowd erupted. The four contestants shook hands with the judges.

"The fix was clearly in." The losing coach spoke bitterly. "We clearly won more total points than Jones/Padilla. I plan to challenge these results." The camera zoomed in on the coach's tirade. "Judge Three was clearly in the Marauders' pocket."

Nothing changed. The New Jersey Links coach even claimed the West Coast bias was in play. The Jersey fans rioted after the contest to show their displeasure swirled for weeks after the event, fueled with countless hours of speculation and endless rehashing of the championship. Fans all over the country chimed in with their opinion, certain that they had the answer for next year, a trade, new ownership, and improved officiating. Argument episodes were analyzed every hour on the hour, looking for the one key to turning around their team's fortunes for the next year.

The school board meeting had gone slowly. The time moved slowly. I mean ice age slow. The time creeps along. The chair droned, reading a report on some report that no one would ever read. I glanced at the clock. It was two minutes since I had looked.

Finally, they were moving into the public comment section, in which people could speak about whatever issue was bothering them. No one ever spoke during this time so I can return to the office and write up the story and get some dinner.

Spoke too soon; there is a whole group of people walking up to speak. They looked like high school students, large builds, must spend a lot of time in the gym. Not sure where in this town, you would find a gym but they were large guys. I wonder what this means.

"We have come here tonight because we believe that the physical skills that we have developed have value. Exercise creates improve health and vigor which leads to greater academic achievement. It provides an opportunity to challenge ourselves in a physical manner.

We would like the board to consider adding a weight lifting class for next fall. It would be a limited enrollment of fifteen students."

There arose a visceral roar of laughter as the student finished his request. The chair spoke, "let's have some order here. Quiet here. Show some decorum." Suddenly, the room was electric. "So, let me see if I understand, clearly. You want the board to authorize a non-academic class so you can exercise?"

"Yes, sir," The kid spoke haltingly.

"That is interesting but highly unlikely, young man." Who gave you such a subversive idea? The concept that you suggest is something that no clear thinking person would offer. Who are your parents?" The question hung in the air, inviting all sorts of thoughts. The student stood, silent. He glanced back at his friends, searching for an answer not only to the question but for a strategy to escape the moment. "The class would prepare us for competition just like the Super Debate."

Another loud roar of laughter punctuated that sentence. He spoke again, "We believe that we should value athletic competition just as we do academic achievement."

The chair spoke quietly but intently. "I have heard enough of this nonsense. These public comment periods are for real issues not this silly stuff." He waved his hand dismissively. "Physical skills and activity has its place in our world. It is an activity that supports our academic pursuits because after all good physical health is necessary to engage in peak academic performance."

He paused again, smiling warmly at the boys at the podium. "I salute your courage in presenting your ideas. But, let us be clear. They are bad ideas. These physical contests do not advance our society. Large crowds confirm the value of academics in our lives. The standard of living, the wealth, the knowledge that our society produces are unprecedented in the history of the world."

He scanned the crowd, looking deeply into eyes of each person. "I am an old man and my time is nearly done." He turned back to athletes. "You will not be allowed to waste this board's time. Refocus your attention on a real future."

The group turned away, heads down. The chair waited until they had left. "Ladies and Gentlemen, this meeting is concluded. The lesson here is that we must remain true to the values that make our society great."

Wow, I thought what a great object lesson for the article. It was a nice angle about young people learning at the hands of the wise chair. He needed to catch those boys and get a quote or two. My editor would love it. I like a great morality ethos for the article. Use the teenagers as an example of wrong thinking corrected dramatically in the meeting through the wisdom of the chair. What a great lesson for those kids and for all of us.

We must do all we can to keep the focus on building a better world. Academics are the key to our future. These kids must learn the lesson.

Jacob stood on the front porch. Dad shuffled his feet, watching his son close up his suitcase.

"You don't have to leave son."

"Yes, I do. You hate me. I will build gyms for people like me. There are a lot of people like me."

"Son, no one cares about this sort of thing. You are doomed to fail."

"Thanks for believing in me Dad."

Jacob closed up the suitcase and they shook hands briefly. His father watched his son walk away. He stood on the porch until his son was no longer in sight. His shoulders dropped when Jacob was gone.

He stood there, silent for a long time.

NEVILLE'S POND

Grace Allison

THE BABY SQUIRRELS will arrive soon. Noel built a soft nest interweaving the fur from her back with twigs, branches, leaves, pine needles, and bird feathers. The young mother was giving birth for the first time.

The crisp smell of fall was in the air. From the tall trees, in a surreal fluttering of leaves, the wind blew the red, orange, and yellow canopy to the forest floor. A full moon, large and orange, set in the southwest corner of Crystal Lake Park. The sunrise was more than pink streaks lighting the eastern sky when Lefty Grendel's 1989 Ford Ranger rattled into the tiny gravel parking lot at Crystal Lake Park.

From her safe home, up in the tall oak tree, Noel heard a dog's angry bark. The sudden bedlam in the early fall morning's quiet startled her. She peeked out a knot hole to see her husband, Neville, running for his life from a black dog whose bark told Neville, "My master wants you tree rats of this wood gone forever."

The devil in hot pursuit, Neville felt the hair on his back stand on end. A little near-sighted without his glasses, his heart beat fast when he missed a tree. He made a quick recovery when he sprang onto the Oak where Noel was building her nest. On his way up the branches, the escapee suffered a sharp tug, heard a snarl, and a snapping sound from the crazy beast whose pointed teeth ripped off a piece of his long, gray tail.

"AAHHH" he screamed in pain and turned to look down to see blood running down his leg. "Where is my tail?" he cried, "How will I jump trees? How will I talk to my friends with my tail? I will be this way forever."

His tail was throbbing and bleeding, Neville's bravery saved his life. In tears, pale and exhausted, his pride and protection snatched by a monster, the new father-to-be begged his wife, "Please, Noel! Please open the door. The mad dog bit me."

Noel felt torn when she considered Neville's dilemma. Her maternal instinct reminded her of what her mother said, "Mother squirrels should let no one near her or her nest until she has given birth."

She pushed her thoughts aside and rushed to rescue him. Then, she saw his mangled tail and the pain in Neville's brown eyes. The morning's attack on Neville made Noel cringe, "Oh, my poor dear. That vicious animal destroyed your beautiful tail." As she bandaged his wound, they listened to a pandemonium happening down near the pond.

The pounding of Lefty Grendel's leather boots along with his mean dog attacking Neville awakened Mack, the Mallard Duck, who squealed at the top of his voice, "Everyone in the wood, beware! Our world is in danger of being destroyed!"

Neville and Noel hurried to listen to their loudmouth friend, "Mack, what is happening?"

Mack loved this wood more than any other place he lived. He flew to many places. The flying traveler reported to Neville and his friends what was happening in the world beyond their lake. Strutting while he quacked, Mack never shuts up. Although he loved to visit other places, he always returned to the quiet grove of trees and his friends. The lake park was his home.

Neville rolled his eyes when Mack quacked. Neville thought Mack was an air-sucking windbag. Until now, the duck's boasting made Neville cringe, but today, maybe it was time to listen to his chatty friend.

Mack, "I have been flying over our town in the last six moons and what were once ponds of water to land in and trees to rest under are now rows and rows of human homes. I think our pond is going away."

Mack handed Neville a copy of the latest daily newspaper. Neville puts on his glasses and reads the story.

"Headlines in the Business Section of *Shady Springs Gazette*.

Crystal Lake Park Sold
Grendel Builders purchased Crystal Lake Park, a ten-acre wetland with its natural spring. The last green belt to survive the cities rapid growth is near downtown Shady Springs, Texas. Shady Springs City Council voted to tighten its fiscal belt and has been selling its vacant properties over the last year. The city could save tens of thousands of dollars from maintenance and upkeep. Crystal Lake Park, the last parcel passed this week to Lefty Grendel of Grendel Builders, whose plan was to build luxury townhomes."

Neville dropped the newspaper in despair and went for a stroll.

There from the tree tops, Neville spotted a caravan of huge yellow trucks with "Grendel Builders" on the vehicle doors heading for the pond. When the crew of six men arrived, they unloaded crates of building materials. Within several hours the workers had installed an 8-foot tall chain-link fence topped with barbed wire all around the wetland. Signs posted on the wall read, "Keep Out No Trespassing."

By the day's end, the horrible escapade and the barricade had torn their peaceful world apart. Neville held his bandaged tail and thought, "Our home is doomed."

The last of the original habitat, Crystal Lake Park, had been an oasis in the middle of a concrete jungle of skyscrapers. On the north side, a winding five-foot wide path meandered through the tall pine, oak, maple, and other trees that surrounded the pond. Often on windy days, a spray of rainbow mist from the 20-foot fountain in the middle of Playa lake showered the ducks.

During their lunch hour, the office workers brought bread to feed the ducks. Neville took home food scraps.

Neville wondered, "What will happen to the visits of humans? Who will bring the golden nuts?" He and his friends waited for the weekly visits of volunteers who brought them corn.

The residents of Shady Springs, Texas, knew Lefty Grendel connived to get what he wanted. During the early days of real estate deals in Shady Springs, Texas Lefty had pulled a knife on his business partner who wanted more than his fair share. In the fight, Grendel's knife had fallen. His partner had snatched it up, slashing Lefty's right eye. A black patch now covered the damage.

Lefty grinned with satisfaction. The barrier trapped all the creatures of the wood in and kept everyone out. Time to head home. Lefty locked the gate and called out, "Scar, get in." He opened the truck door, and the black Labrador jumped into the passenger side. "What do you have in your mouth, a squirrel's tail? Good boy!" Lefty whacked the dog's back in approval, then slammed the truck door shut.

While Lefty was inspecting the lake at his new acquisition, several squadrons of aggressive mosquitos had bitten his arm. On his way home, he rolled up his sleeve and scratched the red welts. Scar reluctantly dropped his prize on the truck seat to bite at his squadron of mosquitos that were bombarding him. The land baron, reflecting on his latest conquest, saw the dollar signs, dancing in his head.

*   *   *

In the following weeks, with the fence in place, the daily activities of the park stopped. A quiet foreboding had swept through the pond. Neville and his friends waited.

A gloomy winter approached. Dark skies and a freezing, blustery rain pelted Crystal Lake Park. Neville had had many neighbors in the Oak-tree nest where he and Noel lived. At the tip of the branch, a Mockingbird family had raised hungry beaks from the seeds that their mother brought. Winter sent the birds to the south to find warmer weather until spring. Neville wanted to stay near Noel until his new family arrived. The empty Mockingbird nest was the perfect temporary resting place.

By the end of March, the warm sun had ushered forth springtime. Tree seedlings were sprouting where Neville and Noel had hidden the acorns.

New hair was growing on Neville's injured tail. He imagined how he'd show his youngsters how to climb and jump from tree to tree.

Noel gave birth and delivered two boys and a girl in her nest. Neville and Noel were celebrating when Mack showed up and said, "Have you read the news?" During the winter, Mack had been spying on Lefty and his dog, ready to warn his friends at the pond. Mack shouted, "The evil man and his dog are dead."

Mack gave a copy of the newspaper to Neville to read. Neville took the paper and read,

"Headlines in the *Shady Springs Gazette*,

West Nile Virus Kills Local

Lefty Grendel, a Shady Springs developer and his dog were found dead by one of his workers yesterday. The Shady Springs the coroner confirmed Grendel and his dog had died from the West Nile Virus. Due to the death of Mr. Grendel, the City of Shady Springs issued a statement dropping the charges of check fraud in the recent purchase of Crystal Lake Park."

In a second story in the *Shady Springs Gazette*, he read,

"City of Shady Springs Donates Wetland

Since the sale of Crystal Lake Park fell through the City of Shady Springs has given the wetland to the Texas Wetland and Waterfowl Association."

Within days of the newspaper article, the Association removed the No Trespassing sign and fence. The Texas Wetland and Waterfowl

Association brought corn for the animals in the park and welcomed the people of Shady Springs, Texas to an Easter Egg Hunt.

New parents, Neville and Noel, made plans for their new family and proclaimed Mack friend and "Park Protector."

Why I Wrote This Story

I wrote this story when real estate developers purchased a protected wetland in Dallas, Texas. The Park was near my home and my daily retreat. One day I walked to the park and found a chain-link fence with a sign that said, "Keep Out No Trespassers."

In shock, my heart sunk. I stared through the interwoven links and imagined the concrete condominiums. So, I wondered what if the animals in the park could talk? What is their story? The animals in the story are anthropomorphic animals that have human characteristics.

CONCHO DIARY

Dale Wender

I T WAS AS close to love as a youngster could imagine.

For years I watched her. I dreamed about her. In a crowded room she saw me. Her face would brighten—oh, there you are. She would walk to me, now relaxing, forgetting her troubles at home. She would drape her arms on my shoulders, touch her forehead to mine.

That never happened. In the usual adolescent fashion I steadfastly avoided eye contact whenever she appeared. I was suddenly busy with my paper, short of breath, heart pounding in my ears, just like true love.

It didn't matter. She wasn't the loving type.

In the 70's I lived in an oil and cattle town you never heard of in the western reaches of the Edwards Plateau. We grew up together, she, myself, and about forty others in our grade, back when the oil rigs still ran and we neither knew or cared about things like changing weather or far away Washington.

Being an only child, everything about girls was mysterious to me. They always had the upper hand. They were the ones desired and pursued. We wanted them; they weren't especially interested in us. They had beauty and grace. They could create life. Their bodies contained sacred and forbidden places. Holy anatomy. They had power, the keys to sex. They were magic, all-knowing, able to stop time.

We boys were either gangly or blockish. What it must have been like for the girls to survey the lot of choices in our school, to consider this one and that one, and eventually resolve to accept one either for dating or for marriage, I cannot imagine. But she was above all that. For all the years that I knew her, on the rare occasions that I became the focus of her distant eyes, she usually assessed me as she would a farm animal.

My home was a three-bedroom shotgun in a neighborhood full of embezzlers, city clerks and Billy-Sunday Baptists.

She lived in a decrepit trailer park— the *Country Aire*—near the highway. CJ, my track partner whose mother worked in the emergency dispatch, once told me in a flagrant breach of confidence that the police had to break up some kind of domestic flap there nearly every week.

Her family was a mess. The turmoil showed in her unkempt fingernails and her erect posture that seemed to overcompensate for something. It showed in her obliviousness to things like movie celebrities and popular footwear, and in her complete disregard for what anyone else thought, which was convenient because nobody else liked her much. Sure, she had a beautiful face. But she was taciturn, and her dewey, guileless gaze was often mistaken for pride.

Like me, she was an only child. We rode the same bus, never speaking. Her neck was thin, especially when we were young; her round head seemed out of proportion. She was not a bright student, but she turned in every assignment. She never looked at the grade. She didn't eat lunch.

But me, I could not stop looking at her. I would always place myself where I could discreetly look at her. I would look beyond her, scratching my chin in thought over some math problem. I learned how to watch her in the foreground or background of whatever I was looking at.

Her expression was like an adult who's having to be patient with you. Her eyelids drooped a little, as if she did not expect anything amazing to happen. The droll mouth almost constantly constrained a beautiful smile, held like a genie in a bottle. Gray eyes, a standard nose; but the devil was in the configuration. What most people marked about her was a perfect spray of tan freckles framed in a blonde haystack of hair. Funny that you don't normally think of a girl with freckles as being the killer.

Occasionally in elementary school PE class, we were required to square dance. Only once was she ever my dance partner. Coach assigned her to me. It was like winning the jackpot.

The square dance caller—bolo tie, western shirt, shiny hair—put the needle on his little 45 record player and the music started. He chanted for us to *promenade*. I felt her torso under her cotton blouse when I put my arm around her; it was glorious and unexpectedly solid. She clutched my hand like a saddlehorn, standing an inch or two taller than me. I whispered sin-drenched prayers to God, pleading for virility. There was no other conceivable occasion in which I could have ever gripped her body this way, nor she my sweating hand. The way lovers do.

I learned that day that she was quite strong. We *do-si-do'ed* with the partner to the right and then she fell back in place at my side with a snap. She turned and pivoted and pulled me into place with a purpose. She sprained my wrist a little.

I dared to touch the supple skin of her inner forearms for an *allemande left*. She did not flinch or withdraw or seem to notice really. She performed the steps like a military drill, spinning me around. She skipped around the circle flouncing strawberry-blonde bundles without care, not smiling either, as if she were completing an assignment. I fantasized that, as my steady girl, perhaps when we were older, I may one day again touch that hairless and supple forearm. She never looked at my face.

By sixteen I was spending most evenings with my gawkish cribmates down under the overpass by the Concho River: CJ, Clem and Scrap. Clem's daddy let him drive their truck, and we set there by the water on his tailgate drinking Pacifico. We'd stop by the red and blue neon lights of Turk's Liquor. His place was outside city limits and the old man never carded.

One evening we were down there talking about girls and the spring rodeo and summer ranching. Someone would always ask Clem how Brio and Hoodoo were holding up and he gave us city boys a lesson in horse's teeth or the mechanics of gelding.

There we sat, everything orange in the sunset, trying to make something of the evening. And she appeared. First we heard, then we saw her fly past in her daddy's old C10 on the opposite bank of the river, speeding alone like she had somewhere to be. We watched in silence. I should be right there, I mused, in her truck, seated beside her, the two of us driving too fast, hitting the gravel shoulder with a shout, two young toughs playing chicken with an invisible car and spitting rocks at any windshield that dared to follow. That's how she always drove: fast, and alone.

She roared by sitting forward on the seat, both hands gripping the wheel the way she did, pushing the limits, that wild hair that never met a comb flailing in the wind. She didn't notice us sitting on the tailgate.

Man oh man, I said. What I wouldn't give.

Fool, said CJ. She's not for you.

As I got older, I tried to show interest in other girls. I spoke to one at the Easter parade. Bought a corsage for homecoming. But nothing ever stuck.

Lately she was only at school about two days out of the week, or so it seemed. Somehow everyone knew her story and nobody talked about it, that she had a fella who sometimes came through town. Velasquez was his name. She wore a thin leather braid around her neck with a vial of some thin liquid inside, a token of his promise. We figured he was running from the law.

I only saw him once near an abandoned graveyard where the two of them were lingering on a cedar fence, tired and distracted like renegade lovers.

Even when she attended school she was seldom in class. I

sometimes saw her drifting alone in some dim corridor. Or by the far exits whispering to the dark-eyed freshman girls who could barely speak English.

My dream was growing restless. I decided I would deliberately get in her path, break into her world. It took some planning. All was quiet, no one else in the hallway. Instead of passing I stepped close to brush her shoulder. I tried to act like I was in her league. But what came out of my mouth, I realized in alarm as the words dropped, sounded more like Velasquez' words than my own.

Hey ol' girl. What's up.

I felt my ears go red. In the awkward silence my lips pressed together in a stiff smile. She stopped and looked up. She seized me by the eyes—the face that I could never not look at now turned to me, her omniscient eyes set behind a veil of dappled, tan spots arranged evenly from temple to temple. This all happened in an instant. The corner of her mouth turned up as we stood there suspended. I read the recognition from our mutual history.

She showed a sort of approval combined with acknowledgement that I had obviously greeted her as a sort of ironic, inside joke. It was the combination of her feral beauty with the gift of her generous, sudden intimacy that slew me. That patient smirk demonstrated that she had confidence upon confidence, personality to spare, an infinite store, that she dispensed her graces freely, that she knew, obviously, as she knew of all young males, what I was thinking in that moment, the entirety of my mental and emotional state, why I'd made the effort to speak to her in the first place. In the lazy and careless wielding of her psychic powers, she knew that I stood there tingling at the simple pleasure of being in the sunbeam of her attention.

She didn't say anything. After ten seconds of unspoken conversation, she chuckled and gave me a firm smack on the arm with the back of her hand, and walked on.

I would never—I now knew—never be what Velasquez was to her.

I'll tell you why. Hadn't she already seen more of life than anyone in our town? The previous summer—aged fifteen—she'd run off. She wanted a vacation, she told, of all people, the school janitor. Never been on a vacation, she said. She vanished and her parents scarcely noticed.

When she reappeared two months later from who knows where new rumors swirled on the wind about Mexican horse traders and a novelist named Carlos Fuentes with whom she had apparently danced and sipped tequila in an unknown mountain village in Chihuahua province. Velasquez had been there. She now wore his onyx ring on her thumb.

I started to feel that I could never keep up with her, that my life was as pedestrian and boring as the whole town's, and her story was on the wind, on the radio, in the glances of all the boys' eyes, was unfolding more every day. She knew all men and found them all more or less the same. Only a man who held even greater mystery, a man like Velasquez, belonged with her.

It doesn't matter now—I don't know why I'm bringing it up. It didn't matter then either.

But we lived together for a while. Here's the story.

When she and I were both twelve she came to live at my house, in our spare room, for one week while her parents sorted out some big scrap that involved a bottle of Everclear, a stolen pistol, and a bedfire in their trailer. It was in the papers for three days. Our church offered to help with the poor girl.

For a week, when I was too young to know what to do with myself, and the knowledge of her proximity more distracting to me than a box of tabby kittens, and my hands suddenly feeling abnormally large, and she being blithely content in her own company, in this state of things, she lived with us.

She sat across from me at the dinner table. While I tried to do homework, she laid on the bed in the spare room next to me, her socked feet up the wall reading mom's old issues of Woman's Day. Or she'd chew gum and pull her bangs cross-eyed on the couch.

Sometimes she left panties, which I had heard about but had never seen, on the floor of the bathroom. Her mystery grew.

As did my ordinariness. She now knew where I lived, how I took out the trash, how I ate my vegetables. About her I only knew that she was from a parallel universe. Unanswered feminine curiosities were a merciless lash to my maniacal raw pubescence.

That week she went with us to church. I wore a thin navy tie and Sunday shoes but she wore the same denim and frayed sneakers she always wore. Mother's missionary smile broadcast the gospel of sartorial tolerance as we entered the building. We tried to act normal.

Midway through the service she whispered something to mother and then left, presumably to go to the bathroom. Suddenly I found it hard to breathe. Mad with curiosity, I waited a minute and then hustled out.

Forgive me Lord. Against all righteousness and decency, I listened at the door to the ladies room. She was not there. I skated down the halls on the toepads of my leather soles. Past door after door of windowless Sunday School rooms, past the empty fishbowl offices. Out the glass doors to the side parking lot. I finally found her in the back by the trash cans in the alley with a couple of other trailer park scamps, arms folded, a cigarette between her fingers.

Again, no words were spoken. I gestured in a manner that asked if she was coming back in, and she nodded in a casual heavy-lidded style that said she'd be back in later. I sat in the pew and didn't hear another word of the sermon until, near the end, she came back in and sat next to me.

I caught her sidelong glance. And she winked at me.

Perhaps a philosopher could justify, although I doubt it, a world where the briefest and most casual flick of the tiniest muscle can bring about the complete psychological breakdown that that wink brought to my soul. Never did an action so fleeting, so provocative, so wanton cause so many years of torment.

We never spoke about the whole event. The next day she returned to her trailer.

The years passed. We boys sat at the riverside and drank Pacifico. It was senior year now. I was going to trade school in a few months. The

Concho was getting low with the years-long drought. I conceded to pursue some other girl lest I be alone forever.

I heard you's taking Millie Starnes to the gala, Clem said.

It's just a fund-raiser, I answered.

Dancing, I hear.

Mm.

We were both envisioning Millie Starnes.

That's some overbite.

Better than sitting here looking at your ugly face.

Then the day came when she vanished for good. I sat in the dark as police lights flashed around the city. Suddenly the dream had never existed. Her disappearance (abduction, suicide, runaway?) was never gotten to the bottom of. The case went cold.

The town shook its collective head at the sad headlines. It was a damn shame, the sheriff said. We, myself far more than anyone else, were stunned—she was human after all. Had she shot herself with the pistol in some canyon? Had Velasquez taken her back to Mexico? Or had she gone to Houston or Dallas, following her mysterious ambitions?

Clem told about spotting Velasquez one day when he was riding Brio. Velasquez was on a horse ranch nearby wearing chaps and running a young paint across the grassland before heading back with the other wranglers for beans and polenta around a fire. She was clearly not run off with him, and that made her disappearance all the more troubling.

Her momma was dead eighteen months, and her daddy's truck stayed parked by his trailer now since he lost his ability to drive. The old man was senseless and generally mournful, but said nothing lucid concerning her whereabouts. They dragged the Concho river bed even though the water was lower than ever. She didn't possess enough belongings to tell if she had packed up or not.

In '79 I had one more semester at the trade school before I was a certified lineman for the county electric cooperative. Clem and I still met under the overpass Fridays to end the work week with a fitting melancholy. The river was a trickle now.

You figuring on marrying Millie? he asked. Maybe work for Judge Starnes?

I don't know.

If she'll have you. Combing that briar patch of yours be a good start.

I opened another Pacifico and spat toward the rivulet.

I reckon Dotty will keep you happy.

About right. Shoot. Did you ever figure me a family man?

I'm sure she'll give you a housefull.

You best show your cards with Millie. She's liable to give up waiting.

I looked across the banks of the Concho and heard a motor roaring. Like that evening years ago, it was an old C10 coming fast, an angular frame clinging close to the wheel as it flew by, spitting up pebbles, reddish-blonde hair whipping in the wind.

And I thought that's where I ought to be, beside her on the bench, hurrying who knows where, if only to escape the heavy stillness of this dusty plateau, to find a place where love is not such an uphill march, not a weakness, not a sunburn, not tearful song.

Why I Wrote This Story

My intention with this story was to try and capture the loneliness, frustration, and melancholy that I felt as a young person. Relationships and longings were alternately euphoric and devastating, and I imagine this was mostly due to my own mediocrity. With this story I want the reader to feel and remember something of that malaise that is the daily experience of youth.

BROKEN PROMISES

Jan Sikes

A TEENAGER IN LOVE with a bright future full of hopes and dreams, Charlotte Lawson stepped out the front door of Central High School and skipped down the steps.

An insistent horn shook her from her reverie.

"Over here, Charley," Damien Blue yelled and waved.

Charlotte glanced around before racing toward the metallic blue Firebird convertible. She tossed her books into the backseat and climbed in. "Wow!" She gasped. "When did you get this car?"

"Just today. I wanted you to have the first ride." He pressed a bouquet of Peruvian Lilies into her hands.

"Oh, Damien." She buried her nose in the fragrant blooms.

He gave her a lopsided grin, jammed the gears and the 1974 Firebird flew down the street. He put a hand on Charlotte's leg. "I've missed you, babe."

"My daddy's gonna kill me," Charlotte muttered.

"What did you say?" Damien kept one eye on the road while he cupped her cheek.

"Oh, nothin'." The tingle from Damien's touch rushed all the way to her toes.

"Don't worry, love. He'll never find out." He turned off the highway onto a country road. "I had to see you."

Charlotte sighed. No one and nothing made her feel alive like

Damien did. But, with bruises from her father's last beating still fresh, she had good reason to worry. Tom Lawson's words still echoed in her mind as he swung the belt. *'I'll not have my daughter hanging around with that no account musician playing the devil's music. Do you hear me?' He'd yelled.*

She shuddered and stared at Damien. His handsome features, shoulder length brown wavy hair, and long lean body would make any girl weak in the knees. But, when he strapped on his guitar . . . oh yeah, that's when he turned into a Rock God.

What a high it had been — going with him when his band opened for The Rolling Stones in Houston two months ago. She got to hang out backstage and watch him perform. He introduced her to all the musicians as his girl. But, meeting Mick Jagger went leaps and bounds beyond her wildest dreams. She'd even gotten her picture taken with him. Her heart beat wildly remembering.

And, that night in the hotel, she'd given herself to Damien in every way.

For a while, every girl in school envied her. That is, until her father put his foot down. Tom Lawson's image, as Deacon in the Baptist church, was more important than his daughter's happiness. He'd made that more than clear and forbade her to see Damien ever again. But, she'd climbed out her window a few days later, after the bruises and whelps healed. Damien waited on the corner.

She loved him, no matter what her father said or did. He couldn't beat her enough to change her heart.

And now, she'd jumped into Damien's car in front of school. There'd be hell to pay if her father found out.

Damien pulled off the road under a spreading oak tree and killed the engine. "Well, what do you think?" He brushed her long blonde hair back with his fingers.

"It's beautiful, Damien." She leaned over the console between them and he claimed her lips.

She craved his tender touch and made no attempt to stop him when he slid his seat back and pulled her onto his lap. He left butterfly kisses on her neck as he unsnapped her bra and pushed her shirt over her head.

"Damien, we shouldn't," she whispered.

"Shouldn't what?" He ran his tongue around a hard nipple. "I need you, Charley. I think about you all the time. Don't you get it? I love you." He murmured against her hot skin.

Oh, she got it alright. Desire, passion, and longing arose from a flame that burned low in her belly. "I love you too, honey." She lowered her head and teased his mouth.

He crushed her against his chest and she parted her lips in invitation. A groan escaped when he hungrily explored the inside of her mouth and his hands gently gripped her hips.

Was it possible for a person to melt and die from desire?

He hit a lever and his seat fell back. She slid over to the passenger side and maneuvered her jeans off while he slipped out of his shirt and pants.

Hell, and be damned! She wanted Damien more than she ever feared her father.

"Come here." He reached for her hand.

His husky voice sent tingles up her spine. She swung on top of him and wrapped her slender legs around him.

A voice inside her head shouted a warning, but it was one she chose to ignore. Her father could do his damnedest to destroy their love, but he would fail.

Later, she lay with her cheek on his chest, her heart beating with his in wild rhythm.

Damien stroked her hair and ran his hands down her back. She winced when he touched a bruise that wasn't yet healed.

"Now that's the way to break in a new car." He chuckled.

She raised her head to meet his blue-gray eyes. "I love you."

"When you turn eighteen, I'm taking you away." He twisted a lock of golden hair around a finger. "And no one can stop me."

She sighed. "I can't wait." She sat up and reached for her clothes. "But, for now, you'd better get me back to town."

While they dressed, Damien told her how popular his band had gotten since they'd opened for The Stones. Excitement filled his words and his eyes sparkled. "Do you know how many guys would give anything to open for those superstars?" He readjusted his seat.

"You earned it, Mr. Rock Star. You're one of the best guitar players in the state."

He caressed her cheek and grinned. "Just another reason I love you, sweetheart. You believe in me."

"You're going to go far, Damien Blue." Charlotte covered his hand with hers.

"And you're going with me, my beautiful golden-haired angel."

"Don't make promises you can't keep," she breathed.

"Never." He kissed her.

She placed a hand at the base of his neck and rested her forehead on his. "You know I have to get back to town."

"I know. Dammit, our stolen moments are always so short." He turned the key and the engine purred like a kitten.

She let the warm breeze blow her worries away on the open highway.

When they neared town, Damien asked, "Where do you want to go, sweetheart?"

"Lindsey's. I'll tell my dad I was studying with her."

"You might want to brush the tangles out of your hair before you try that story, my love." He laughed.

He stopped in front of a two-story house with lilacs blooming by the porch. "See you soon?" He put a finger to her lips.

"I promise." She grabbed her books from the backseat and jumped out. She stood at the curb and watched until she could no longer see the flashy blue Firebird.

Weeks passed and she managed to see Damien a few more times without her father's knowledge.

In the meantime, Tom Lawson had introduced Charlotte to a young intern at his law firm, Arthur Peters. She knew exactly what her father was up to and played along with the charade. But, nothing would change her heart. She loved Damien. She'd bide her time.

After all, she'd be eighteen soon and then she could leave and put the nightmare behind her.

Charlotte overheard conversations in the hallways at school about Damien Blue and how popular he was becoming. Everyone predicted he'd hit the big time soon. She hoped it wouldn't be until she was free to go with him. But, she kept quiet and listened to the chatter. Only her closest friends knew she still saw Damien, and they were sworn to secrecy. They'd seen the bruises and whelps her father had left on her and vowed to protect her.

When Damien told her he would be opening for The Allman Brothers Band in two weeks, she knew she had to go.

She confided in Lindsey and they made a big deal about a sleepover at her house that Saturday night.

A foolproof plan, Damien was to pick her up at Lindsey's on Saturday afternoon and have her back early Sunday morning.

Saturday came and Charlotte was as jittery as a long-tailed cat in a room full of rockers. She'd avoided her parents until time for Lindsey to pick her up. She agonized over what to wear. Suede bell-bottom pants, four-inch clogs and turquoise and tan silk blouse with fringe around the yoke won out. She packed them into the bottom of her bag and laid her pajamas and another change of clothes on top, in case her father decided to inspect.

Shortly after noon, Lindsey honked. Charlotte flew out of her bedroom and threw a goodbye over her shoulder.

"Just a minute." Her father stopped her.

She turned to meet his glare. "You know what happens when you lie to me."

"Lindsey and I are just going to a movie tonight. See you tomorrow."

"I'll be checking up on you."

"I'll see you and mom tomorrow."

Her mother smiled weakly and waved. Funny how she'd never questioned why her mother didn't try to intervene in the beatings. Maybe she was as scared of Tom Lawson as Charlotte. She flung the thoughts aside. Her heart pounded as she raced toward Lindsey's car.

Once inside, she hugged her friend. "I can never thank you enough,

Lindsey. I know you could get into big trouble for this, but at least your dad doesn't beat you."

Lindsey put the car in gear and pulled away. "I'm glad to do it, Charley. It's not right that he keeps you and Damien apart."

The girls chattered and Charlotte filled her friend in on all the details including her father's threat to check up on her.

"Don't worry. I'll handle it, if he does," Lindsey assured.

At two o'clock sharp, Damien pulled up in front of Lindsey's house. The girls were waiting on the porch and Charlotte hugged her friend, then with her heart racing, she ran to the man she loved.

Damien kissed her and placed two fragrant Peruvian Lilies in her hair.

Only an hour drive to the concert venue, they sang along with the radio while flying down the highway.

Once there, Charlotte stayed out of the whirlwind of setup, sound check, last minute rehearsal and song changes. Damien occupied her thoughts while she fetched beer or bottled water.

When the Allman Brothers Band arrived, they showed nothing but respect toward Damien. Something clenched her gut. Would she lose him to the life and career he seemed destined to have?

Could he be serious about wanting to take her along? She knew beyond any doubt she'd follow him to the ends of the earth.

The young budding attorney, Arthur Peters, was nice enough, but she'd never had the slightest urge to kiss him. The closest he'd gotten to kissing her was a peck on the cheek.

No, it was Damien Blue who set her blood on fire.

The night flew by. The music, partying and lovemaking lasted until the wee hours of morning.

Charlotte fell asleep with her head on Damien's shoulder.

She awoke in a panic and fear gripped her. One look at the clock in the motel room told her she was in big trouble. Her head pounded from the alcohol and when she moved, she groaned. The lilies from her hair lay crushed in pieces on the tangled sheets.

She shook Damien. "Wake up!"

He turned over and groaned.

She shook him again. "Damien! Honey, you have to wake up!"

He rolled over and raked a hand across his eyes. "What's wrong, babe?"

"It's already past noon. I have to get back to Lindsey's."

He reached for her. "Oh shit! I'm so sorry."

She threw back the covers. "My father will be furious."

"Don't worry, sweetheart. I'm going to take care of you."" He jumped to his feet. "Damn! My head is pounding."

Charlotte ran to the motel room coffee pot and set it brewing while she slipped into her clothes. She wished she'd thought to bring a change with her. But, she hadn't planned on needing one.

"Here." She pressed a Styrofoam cup in Damien's hand. "Let's go."

She bit her fingernails and watched the speedometer climb to over one hundred. Maybe she'd make it.

While he drove, she memorized every line in his face. If she never saw him again, it would be etched forever in her mind.

Somehow, she knew deep inside she would lose him. Not to another girl, but to music. Watching him perform last night left no doubt it was his true passion. The fact that he was getting more offers to open for rock's heavy hitters, pretty much assured he'd soon be the one someone else would be opening for.

He turned onto Lindsey's street and Charlotte cried out. "Oh my God! You can't stop. That's my dad's car."

She swiped at tears that wouldn't stop. What had she done? She'd blown everything.

Damien hit the dash with his fist. "This is bullshit. I'm going to go in and have it out with him right now. What he does to you is wrong."

"No! Please," Charlotte begged. "It would just make it worse."

"Then what do you want me to do?" he growled.

She looked at him and he reached for her trembling hand. "Take me home," she whispered.

He passed Lindsey's house and kept going. "I'm not going to stand by and let him lay another hand on you."

"Just take me home and I can at least get cleaned up and changed out of these clothes before he gets there."

Damien's frown deepened. "Charley, I don't like this. Come to my place until he simmers down — for as long as it takes."

"You don't know my dad." She wrung her hands. Tears clogged her throat and she wanted more than anything to believe him.

"You're right. I don't know him, but I've seen the bruises he's left on you and I'm not going to drop you off and drive away. I can't do it."

"What else can I do?" Charlotte wrung her hands.

"Come with me to my pad, honey. At least until we can figure this out."

She nodded and her shoulders heaved with sobs. Wooden legs carried her inside Damien's apartment. What was she going to do? She couldn't stand another beating. But, if she didn't go home, her father would use his clout as an attorney to have her and Damien arrested and jailed. She couldn't let that happen.

They collapsed on the sofa and Damien put an arm around her. She rested her head on his shoulder and sniffled.

"Honey, there's something I need to tell you." He stroked her hair.

"What?" she muttered.

"Last night, The Allman Brothers' manager pulled me aside and made an offer I can't refuse."

She sat up and faced him. "What kind of offer?"

"He wants to start booking me."

"I hope you said yes. You know you have to do it." She wiped her eyes. "Oh, baby, I'm so proud of you."

"But, there's something else." He glanced away. "I can't take you with me. I'm sorry," he said softly.

Her heart plunged to her toes and her stomach twisted in knots. There it was. "I can't live without you, Damien."

"It'll only be for a little while. By the time you finish school, I'll be back, love." He pulled her into the circle of his arms.

She shook her head. "No, you won't. You think you will, but you won't. You'll meet all kinds of beautiful women on the road and you'll forget I exist."

He stroked her hair. "I could never forget you, my golden-haired angel. Not even if I tried, and believe me I won't try. But, I've gotta grab this opportunity."

"Of course, you do." She touched his cheek. "It might never come along again." Charlotte drew in a deep breath and pushed to her feet. "I need to go home."

"You sure?" Damien stood and wrapped his arms around her.

Her words fell flat. "Yeah, I'm sure."

"Will I see you again before I leave on tour?"

"I don't know. I'll try." Even though she tried to be happy for him, she couldn't make her voice convincing. Her world had shattered. The whippings her father had given were nothing compared to the beating her heart was taking.

A few minutes later, Damien pulled up in front of her house. He leaned over and kissed her cheek. "I love you, Charley."

"I love you too," she choked. "And I always will."

She opened the car door and shuffled up the walk. How she longed to run back and tell him she was pregnant with his baby. But, she couldn't be the one responsible for squashing his dreams. She wouldn't be that person.

She walked past her mother's inquisitive stare without speaking and went straight to her bathroom. Hot water running over her head helped clear her thoughts and she'd barely gotten dried off and dressed before she heard her father's thunder.

No matter what, she'd not take another beating. She'd tell him everything. He wouldn't hit her if he knew she was pregnant.

Two months later, on her eighteenth birthday, Charlotte stood in front of the Justice of the Peace with Arthur Peters and vowed to stay by his side until death parted them.

Damien's baby growing inside her deserved a good life and Arthur could give that to the child.

She'd be the best wife possible, and maybe in time, even grow to care for him.

She wouldn't make any promises.

Because, promises were only made to be broken.

The End

Why I Wrote This Story

"Broken Promises" is the backstory to a novel I recently finished about Charlotte and Damien's child, Jag Peters. I needed to tell her story so the readers could understand her motivations for what she did. I will use it as part of my marketing for the new book once it is published.

HEART OVER MIND

Ernie Lee

S CHOOL LET OUT early for some reason. I didn't know why, nor did I care very much. I could hear Momma and Grandma arguing all the way out back to Jack's pen. Jack was what we called a brindle in those days. He would probably be called a pit bull today, but we hadn't heard that term in South Texas in the 1950s. He was a big fellow, easily forty pounds heavier than my skinny self. His big old head was square and his massive jaws were black lipped. He had large brown eyes that always looked sad. He always seemed to me like he was trying to tell me something.

Jack belonged to my Uncle Jess who kept him in grandma's back yard. Uncle Jess wanted Jack to be mean for some reason. Someone stole something from him once, and Uncle Jess wanted to make sure that the next person who came up into the yard would pay. Every time he saw that dog he would slap Jack across the jowls, and grab his snout and roughly shake it back and forth until the dog got angry and began to growl and slobber. Jack hated Uncle Jess, and pretty soon he would growl and get tense any time Uncle Jess came around. But Jack never bit Uncle Jess—not even once.

After a few months of rough treatment, Jack got so mean no one could come around him but me. He'd let me sit beside him after school and pet his neck and rub his shoulders. Anytime anyone else came around, he would jump up and start growling and the hairs on his back would stand up stiff. But, when no one else was around, he was calm, like when he was a puppy and would look at me with those big brown eyes like he was trying to tell me how mean everyone was to him. He'd growl and bare his teeth at me sometimes especially if I got close to his face, but he never bit me or even tried.

I got closer to the house to see what the fight was about this time. They didn't hear me come through the back screen. Momma and Grandma were in the dining room going at it, both faces contorted into rage and both yelling at the top of their lungs.

"You can't just up and run off to Galveston anytime you want to!" Grandma said. "You got kids."

Momma didn't like to be told no. She cursed and shouted, "Look! I work my ass off every day for my kids, and I want to go to Galveston on the weekend to go fishing and have some fun. I don't get any fun anymore! I'm going!"

"And hang out with Bob!" Grandma sneered.

"What of it? I'm divorced, and Bob is good to me, and he's good to my kids!"

"Yeah, you're divorced for the second time! Well, it's your kids you should be thinking of more!"

"Kids! Kids! Damn kids! I should have stayed divorced that first time! I wish I didn't have no more kids!"

The slap sounded like a gunshot going off! Momma's sunglasses flew across the room and skidded to my feet.

"DON'T YOU EVER let me hear you say that!" Grandma was yelling. "That boy idolizes you -- he worships the ground you walk on! Those kids love you."

I reached down and picked her sunglasses off the floor. An audible gasp came out of both of them as I walked into the dining room to hand the shades to Momma. The screaming stopped. Momma took the glasses and with tears streaming down her face mouthed the words, "I'm sorry." Then, with her hand covering the slap marks on her left cheek, she looked back and forth between me and Grandma, and ran out of the house, got into her red '57 Chevy, and roared off. To Galveston, I guess.

I stood in the doorway watching her leave. Grandma came up behind me and laid her hand on my shoulder. "Bo, people say things when they're mad and hurt that they don't really mean. You know that. She didn't mean what she said, she was just upset. She'll be back."

After I changed out of my school clothes and put my shoes away, I pulled on my old blue jeans and a t-shirt and headed for the back door.

"Bo, I want you to stay away from Jack from now on."

"Why, Grandma?"

Her hard gray eyes flashed as she fixed me with a stare. I knew she didn't like to be questioned, but I also knew she'd let me get away with it. She didn't smile, she rarely did, her features solemn. Her pure white hair, piled high on her head, was impossibly bright in the Texas sun. Sometimes she looked just like an old Indian squaw—but you knew better than to call her that.

"'Cause I told you to, that's why." It was her stock answer.

"But, Grandma! Me and Jack are friends. I might be the only friend he has left in this whole world."

"Bo, Jack is a dog. He don't know the difference from a friend from nothin' anymore. Jess has made him into a mean watch dog, and when you go inside his territory he will protect it. He'll hurt you bad one day. And, I can't have that."

"Oh, Grandma, Jack would never hurt me. I've been his friend forever. He loves me. And I love him, and I can't just quit pettin' him. I would break his heart. He wouldn't understand that. He'd think the whole world was against him."

"Bo! That dog don't love nobody or nothing—not you, nor Jess, or anyone. He's been trained to hate people, and you are people. He's almost twice your size and he could break your neck in an instant. You stay away from that dog. I'll make Jess move him out behind the barn tonight. You stay away from back there, you hear?"

I knew there was no use to argue. "Yes, ma'am."

She didn't smile, but her eyes crinkled like when I said something funny. She reached out and put her hand on the back of my neck and took me inside. A big, old, black fan was whirling on the ceiling of the dining room, as she opened the ice box. She pulled out a Dr. Pepper which she always drank in the late afternoon. "Come on, you can have a sip of my pop," she said, "before the others get here."

It was our secret. Grandma and I had lots of secrets; like the fact that I was her favorite grandchild. She had over thirty of them, but she never shared her pop with any of them—just with me so far as I knew. The cold soda burned as it went down and brought tears to my eyes. Dr. Pepper just doesn't taste the same these days as it did back then. Then it was stronger and not as sweet. You could taste the flavors better then than you can now. We didn't have soda pop on a regular basis—just on holidays or big family gatherings. Those were my favorite times. They would fill up a big old wash tub with ice and there would be hundreds of bottles in that cold, icy water. With an unguarded tub, we'd drink as many as we could fish out. We'd run around with our hands and fingers half frozen, chunking gobs of ice at each other. A different tub would hold the beer. There would be smoky, grilled meat and hand-cranked ice cream. We lived for those days. But this wasn't one of those days. I'd have to be satisfied with just one sip. Grandma snatched the bottle back and swatted me on the bottom, and shooed me toward the back door.

"You remember what I told you, Bo!—about Jack."

"Yes, ma'am."

She grabbed me by the collar of my t-shirt, turned me around, and eyed me closely. "I know you. You'll give me that smile of yours and say, 'Yes, ma'am', but I know you are going to do it anyway—just you be careful and don't let that dog get ahold you! That chicken pen ain't far enough away! I'm going to have Jess haul that dog off tonight!"

"Yes, ma'am."

"Yes, ma'am!" She mocked me in her version of my voice as I swung out the back door. I could feel her worried eyes follow me into the yard. Grandma knew me better than even Momma did. Grandma never said anything she didn't mean, and I was sure Jack's days in the backyard were down to zero. He was a goner!

I knew Uncle Jess would not be home until late. He was out drinking beer and playing dominoes, and wouldn't even show up for supper. I also knew Grandma was watching me from the kitchen window. So I didn't even look at Jack as I sidled around the corner where I knew Grandma couldn't see me. Just to be sure, I reached up into the plum tree and shook a limb like I was after the tart, green plums.

"Stay out of that plum tree, Bo!" came wafting through the air from the direction of the house. I knew she was watching. "You'll get worms! Go feed the chickens!"

I went through the gate in the hog wire fence and headed to the barn. I swung open the rickety door in the crib and opened the corn bin. I filled the coffee can with maize and corn mix and went into the chicken yard, spreading the seed as I walked. The chickens flocked around and pecked the ground around me. I hated chickens! I hated the way they smelled, and how they flocked around trying to beat each other out of the feed, even though there was enough for all of them. I hated the way the soft, warm, chicken shit squeezed up between your toes. I hated the way it crusted up and got hard on your feet if you didn't get it off right away. It was nasty! I went and stood in the water trough until my feet were clean. The cold water felt good on my feet, and I looked around for a patch of grass that didn't have sticker burrs to hop into so I wouldn't get my feet muddy.

I stood on the green grass until my feet were dry, and then went back toward the barn to take the coffee can back. The crib door swung shut behind me, and I sat down on the wooden feed box. The sun was shining brightly outside, but inside the stuffy crib, it was dim. The old tin on the side of the crib was full of old nail holes and tears, and streamers of beams shimmering through the holes splashed onto the walls and the hard dirt floor. Some of those old nail holes were so old they were from square nails! I noticed for the first time that a sunbeam was almost always round or circular regardless of the shape of the hole it passed through. They were like dozens of tawny soda straws filled with pure light. You could see the bright, square, nail hole full of light, but the beam falling to the floor seemed roundish. Whenever they hit a surface, they changed back into the original shape. I didn't know why, but Grandma said things were not always like they seemed. The light wasn't pure either, I could see little specks of dust floating in the soda straws.

I went out the back of the crib on the barn side and walked down to the path leading to little dry creek behind the house. I remembered the cousins and my sisters should be home by now, so pretty soon there would be someone to play with. So instead of going to the creek, I decided to turn back and wait for them, so I headed back toward the house.

As I passed the side yard, Jack saw me and wagged his tail. Just to be sure, I heaved a rock against the side of the barn. When Grandma didn't holler at me I figured she was busy herding the other kids out of their school clothes and supervising the girls in the kitchen or something. I went over and sat down by Jack and cradled his head in my lap. He seemed glad to see me—he didn't growl at all.

"Hey! Jack, boy! How are you, buddy? See! You're glad to see me too, ain't you? You like ole Bo, don't you? You are a good boy, ain't you?"

Jack rolled over on his back for me to scratch his belly, then he rolled the rest of the way over so I could scratch his back. His big brown eyes were full of love, and I just knew in my heart he'd never hurt me. I laid my head on his dusty back and knew that this might be the last time I'd ever see him. Jack squirmed around and licked my face, making those little whimpering sounds he always made. He was trying to tell me he loved me.

Suddenly, I don't know why, but I decided to hug his neck. I grabbed for his head but missed and brushed against his tender snout instead. He clamped down with those massive jaws on my left hand, and I heard a sickening crunching sound and felt blinding pain! Blood shot out of an ugly gash on my hand. Bright red blood was coming out pretty fast, and I went running, screaming toward the house. I ran headlong into Grandma coming out the back door. She took one look at my hand and wrapped it up in a dishtowel and put me in the pickup and drove me to the hospital.

They got the bleeding stopped, gave me a shot right in the middle of the bite, and I got four stitches in my hand. It wasn't broken, but it hurt like the dickens. Grandma had a few choice words about that "damned dog" and Uncle Jess as she drove home. She walked me into the yard and told me to go inside and lay down. After about what seemed like an hour, I got up. The sun was sinking in a yellow gold haze of a south Texas late spring. Grandma was sitting on the porch in her chair.

"You ok?"

"Yes, ma'am."

"Took a hunk out of you, didn't he?"

"Yes."

I looked and saw she had the .410 shotgun across her lap. I knew it was the one she kept behind the front door. I had shot it many times at squirrels and rabbits down by the creek.

"Bo, you have to go shoot that dog."

"What? Grandma, I can't do that. I can't shoot Jack!"

"You have to, Bo. He ain't Jack no more. Quit calling him Jack. He's just a dog!"

"Why?"

"'Cause he bit you bad. He's got to be shot, and I thought you'd want to be the one to do it rather than someone else. What if he gets your sister next time—or the baby? What if he breaks your neck next time? He's tasted blood now, and he ain't afraid of people no more. He won't hesitate to do it again. You know that."

She handed me the gun. "It's loaded. Now go on out there and shoot him before it gets dark."

"I don't want to shoot him, Grandma!"

"Boy! I know you don't! Sometimes a man has got to do things he don't want to do! This is one of them times! No go do it, and dig a hole and put him in it and cover him up."

She pushed the gun into my hands, and I took it and went around the corner of the house. My stomach was doing flip flops, and I felt like I was going to puke. That old gun felt so heavy. I had carried it to the creek and back a hundred times and it never felt that heavy— seemed like it weighed a hundred pounds. I wanted to drag it behind me like a dead weight. Jack sat chained in the yard by the tree wagging his tail at me, and looking at me with those big brown eyes. I propped the gun against a Chinaberry tree and just stood there looking at him knowing what I had to do. I was turning over in my mind that maybe I could unchain him and chase him away down to the creek, but I knew he would just come back. Tears welled up. There was no way out. I had to shoot him—Grandma said. I was overcome with the compulsion to touch him one more time.

Suddenly there was an explosion that sounded right next to my head. It almost blew my ear drums out. At first, I thought the gun had fallen over and went off. Jack lurched up and yelped and fell back dead, a gaping hole in his chest—blood pouring out of him. I turned around and saw Grandma with the gun in her hands; a cloud of blue-gray smoke was curling out of the barrel.

"Grandma! I was gonna do it!"

"I know you were. I also know you were going to keep loving that old dog if he gnawed your arm plumb off. I can't have that. I had to shoot him before you got close enough for him to bite you again."

"I thought if I could love him enough, it'd be ok—he'd be ok."

I looked up into eyes the color of the gun smoke that curled around her face and saw the love she had for me, and I felt her fingers curl behind my neck as she pulled me to her. She smelled like Grandma.

"Bo . . . You can't make somebody love you—they either do or they don't. It don't really matter much what you do because it ain't about you. It's about them—it's what's in their heart, not yours."

She handed me a shovel and turned away so I couldn't see her eyes anymore. "Finish the job. Go dig a hole and put him in it." She turned and went back to the house—I watched her go. Halfway to the house, she shifted the .410 to her other hand, and I thought she wiped her eyes with her apron, but maybe it was just sweat.

I cried the entire time I dug Jack's grave. I wasn't crying for Jack. I cried because of what Grandma said.

My mind said she was right. But, in my heart, I knew she was wrong.

Why I Wrote This Story

The story is a composite story of growing up in the 1950s in south central Texas. Descriptions of my grandmother are as I remembered her and our relationship. I was recording some of my thoughts about those days when I remembered some of the things she used to say and do. Many times, you can know something is true in your mind, but in your heart, you do not want to believe that. When the heart and the mind are in conflict, I always go with my heart. I think a lot of people have those same conflicts.

EARLY WANDERINGS AND UNHOLY REVELATIONS

Darlene Prescott

I

I grew up in an oil refinery town near Houston. When I graduated from high school, in 1964, I was supposed to marry and have children. Accept my fate. There was an appropriate young man who was willing to have me. But I knew somehow that was not for me.

I began wandering, both physically—and mentally.

Without any advice or structure, I dabbled in all kinds of knowledge, first studying anthropology at the University of Texas. I once had read that individuals who are attracted to anthropology are more likely to be "observers of life," rather than those who jump right into the mess. I would be the first to admit that I've always been an introvert—more interested in ideas than accumulating friends, or husbands.

While at UT, I took courses on the world's religious systems, writing papers on women's place in them. Not wholly unexpected, there was a pattern: woman's (undeserved) second-class status was sanctified by religious doctrine and institutions. It did not matter if she was a native of Indonesia or Switzerland.

Even as a child, being indoctrinated into rather undemanding Protestantism, I had become suspicious of religion. If Adam and Eve were the first living beings on the planet, then how did prehistoric dinosaurs fit into the picture? Did Eve really bring sin into the world and, therefore, had to be punished with painful childbirth and obedience to her husband—because she wanted knowledge? Why did all females—who married and/or gave birth— have to be punished?

Without realizing it at the time, my formal studies were substantiating my early suspicions.

II

Just after I earned my anthropology degree, my roommate, Marcie, exclaimed one evening that she would go to Europe if she could find someone to go with her. I heard myself saying, "I'll go." Within six months, we had hopped on a plane to New Orleans—my first plane trip—and the next day we were on a cargo ship—also a first.

Our ship had accommodations for half a dozen paying passengers, who took their meals in the officers' mess. I think the Captain fancied Marcie. I got seasick. But I quickly recovered, and Marcie was able to avoid the Captain for the 14-day sea voyage. Travel was not risk free, but hazards were part of a growth process inherent in adventure.

It was 1967, and, while we were on the high seas, the Six Day War broke out in the Middle East. Our first stop was to be Algiers, where a cargo of beans was to be offloaded at the port. But we received a message from the American shipping company that owned our ship that we should skip that docking. The U.S. was politically aligned with Israel, and we could have found ourselves in trouble in the Arab city.

Nothing new with religious wars. Such wars have plagued human history for thousands of years, and, no doubt, will continue. Today, the Northern Ireland "troubles"—between the Catholics and Protestants—have subsided, but modern Middle Eastern "holy wars" simmer, erupt, and expand.

Our ship sailed on to Barcelona. Marcie and I left the ship in the Italian port of Genoa and began touring the continent with eyes wide open. I have returned to Europe many times, but those first impressions are so much more vivid in my mind.

I don't know if Marcie shared my awakening wanderlust. Now that

I look back, Marcie probably was running away from her Mississippi small-town culture. I was walking towards new experiences. The two of us, however, did get on well, but our paths did part at one point.

Marcie ended up getting married, in Gibraltar, to a former police officer from what was then Rhodesia. She had met him while we were staying in a small Spanish town on the Costa Blanca. There were other expatriates in the fishing village of Campello. We spent our days eating potato omelets and drinking Cuba Libres in the local cantinas, lying on the beach, and going to bull fights. The sun was warm and comforting.

It was time for me to head back up to England.

My most serious entanglement was with Mitchell, a young American man I met in London. I was working as a waitress in one of London's first American-style hamburger places, the Yankee Doodle, and he and his buddies would come in for a meal. They were working for the U.S. Naval Intelligence. Yes, there was a Naval Intelligence office in London—in an unmarked building near the U.S. Embassy.

We would discuss the Vietnam War, in full force at the time, and spend nights at the London Playboy Club. This was before I realized I was a feminist!

Eventually, I returned home, after almost a year. Not surprisingly, I had changed. I wondered what happened to Mitchell, after I wrote and told him that I would not marry him. I had not changed completely. There definitely was something in the back of mind warning me that a family would limit my serious meandering.

III

The Israeli connection again materialized. I had met an Israeli seaman in a Houston disco one night. He would travel to Houston regularly as First Mate with an Israeli cargo shipping company. The cargo ship connection also showed up!

I liked Ariel well enough. Soon he invited me to visit him and his mother in their home in Jerusalem. I saved some money and flew to Israel. That was my first look at that ancient land.

Ariel showed me around in his old Mercedes, and his mother served up delicious meals from her old Yemenite Jewish recipes.

One of Ariel's brothers was a detective on the Jerusalem police force—so I got an earful. Not so much about the local Palestinians, but more about how some of the more conservative Jewish groups caused problems for the larger population. If you run a wire across a public road to prevent travel on the Sabbath, those motorcyclists who ride on that road risk serious injury or death.

After my return to Houston from the Holy Land, I began going from one lousy job to another. I knew I was not accomplishing anything. I thought I might go for my master's, but couldn't make up my mind. I knew I didn't want to teach. I always had been a positive type, but during that time I felt lost. I had to do something.

IV

I flew to New York City. It was 1977. I took off not knowing a soul in the Big Apple. My mother thought I would be back in a few weeks. I returned home 28 years later.

New York suited me just fine. I explored every nook and cranny of that complex metropolis and took advantage of its many opportunities. I landed a job at the United Nations. I started at the bottom, as a typist in the press typing pool. By the time I retired from the U.N., I had earned a law degree and become a legal officer in the international organization, but that is another story.

The United Nations was a good match for me. I could work with people from around the world—find out about them. I also could move around the vast U.N. system, soaking up as much as I wanted. Soon, I volunteered and was assigned to the U.N. Interim Force in Lebanon—better known by its acronym, UNIFIL. This peacekeeping mission was mandated to keep peace between Israel and Lebanon. UNIFIL remains in place.

I was back in Israel. As far as I know, I don't have any Semitic ancestry, but the Middle East kept revealing itself to me. But, then again, Christianity was born in the Middle East—out of the same culture as its "relatives," Judaism and Islam.

In those days, UNIFIL international civilian staff lived in Nahariya, in northern Israel, and we would cross the Israeli-Lebanese border each workday, as UNIFIL headquarters is located just inside Lebanon at Naqoura. The military staff, from a number of countries, lived at headquarters, and the local civilian staff lived in a Lebanese village up the road. The CIA types stayed here and there.

My old Israeli friend, Ariel, had left Jerusalem some time ago and moved to California. I think he married a German flight attendant. There was so much more to discover this trip, not only in Israel, but also in the nearby countries that I knew I would visit. There was one archaeological site after another to explore, museums to visit, and cafes to sit in.

I came to realize that traveling is liberating—as I racked up unique experiences and gained knowledge not necessarily available elsewhere. I found that I could more freely question sacred cows—and bulls.

While traveling is liberating, female travelers in the Muslim Middle East have to be more cautious and, in many cases, have to submit to the restrictive customs imposed on Muslim women.

There also are restrictions on women in the Jewish and Christian worlds. She doesn't have to wear an abaya to cover herself, but similar to her Muslim sisters she is frequently discriminated against in the workplace because of her gender—and legally can be prevented from taking the top jobs in religious institutions. And millions of women appear to have accepted this restriction—giving loyalty and money in support of those male-privileged religious bastions. Why don't women create their own religions?

Anne was sympathetic to my concerns. She had come from the London U.N. Information Office, also to work with UNIFIL. Wanderlust, however, had not brought Anne to the mission. It was for personal reasons.

One day, Anne and I decided to make a road trip to Baalbek in the

Beqaa Valley, in northeastern Lebanon. There are magnificent Roman ruins in Baalbek, and we wanted to see them.

We had the necessary paperwork processed, borrowed a UNIFIL jeep, and set out one Saturday morning. As we crossed the bridge over the Litani River, we were royally saluted by young, armed PLO men standing guard. You would have to have been there to appreciate the humor of that situation. These days, the Hezbollah might be hanging about.

We continued on toward the Beqaa Valley, cars passing us on both sides. There were no traffic cops in that part of Lebanon. After checking into the hotel in the town of Palmyra, we headed over to the ruins.

That part of the world has a long history of wars. It was in 47 BCE that Julius Caesar conquered the area and established the ancient Roman religious system of Jupiter, Mercury, and Venus, replacing what went before in the area. Those gods, and goddess, were celebrated as a holy trinity. The beautiful temple site in Baalbek is what is left of those days.

In today's Middle East, the one-male God of Judaism, Christianity, and Islam is worshipped. Standing there, however, before those grand ruins, one had to acknowledge that the ancient devotees had to be just as sincere in their beliefs as are worshippers of current religions.

Anne turned to me and remarked, "I wonder why religion has played such an important role in human history?"

I could have gone into a discussion about the anthropological and psychological theories I had come across in my studies for explaining religious belief, but, instead, I merely said: "Well, I'm not sure, but whatever the reasons, religions will continue to change shape, reflecting what is going on in the larger culture."

I drifted back to my thoughts. What religions would I find if I could travel far into the future? Perhaps the urge to attribute sin to women would have diminished, as had the "need" for human and animal sacrifices! Perhaps some other form of spirituality would emerge down the road—one that did not require worshipping anything—including an anthropomorphic goddess or god.

Well, Anne and I saw the ruins, contemplated the human condition, and returned to UNIFIL headquarters—without a scratch on us or on the jeep.

V

My later wanderings around the world—and universities—have been equally illuminating and rewarding. I am glad that I got an early start.

Why I Wrote This Story

We have all been told not to talk about politics and religion in polite company. Well, perhaps it is time to chuck that old rule, especially when those human inventions are used to deny basic human rights to half the Earth's population. While my story is not wholly about the rights of women, it is an important part. Generally, I feel I have been fortunate to have had some interesting adventures, and simply wish to share with others. Storytelling, of course, has been part of human culture from our earliest days—and probably began before the practice of any religion.

SWISH, SWISH—THE MISTAKE

Renne Siewers

L IFE WAS SIMPLER in the 1950's, but I knew both women and men were watching me and my beautiful young daughter. We walked down the streets of the dusty Texas neighborhood as my starched slip slowly swished back and forth. The slip rubbed against my legs making that swishing noise. Their eyes fixated as we passed, but they did not speak. It had always been like that since I had my baby girl. We were on our way to the library for me to study. I was finishing up my high school degree.

I said to my sweet daughter, "Don't you give them no mind. They have nothing better to do."

Their glares still surprised me each time I walked past. I wanted to shout and scream at them. "She is no different than you are."

But the truth of the matter, my sweet daughter was. Some would say, "She is a Melato." The parents said, "Children, don't have anything to do with that child. She's not like us. She's a mixture of her colored Momma and white Daddy. The child is evil with white blood."

Neither white nor colored folks wanted to have anything to do with us. My heart broke each time I looked into my child's eyes. How could I make such a mistake?

My daughter just didn't know who her Daddy was. She was the prettiest little girl around. Her eyes glimmered and sparkled with deep blue as you would find in the ocean. Her skin was pure bronze color. Her smile lightened our way as she waved to the people who ignored her. This did not stop her from waving each day.

She often asked about Daddy and how we met. I couldn't tell her the truth at her age but I ran through the story in my head as I walked.

Well, his car broke down a couple miles back from the house. I believe he was a traveling salesman. No one came into these parts unless they were lost, especially a white boy. He walked up to our door.

My Daddy met him at the door and asked, "What do you want?

The stranger said, "I'm having trouble with my car. Can you help me?"

We were about to sit down to dinner, so I quickly asked, "Can we share our food with him?"

Mom was a Christian woman and said, "Of course."

She had made a big pot of beans with ham hocks and cornbread. He sat down and ate them like there was no tomorrow.

Daddy said in a slow Texas drawl, "It's late, so I guess you can spend the night on the couch. The first thing in the morning we will go look for your car. We will have day light and be able to see to fix it. We can't work on the car in the dark now, can we?"

I thought it was odd Daddy let him sleep inside, since I had never seen a white person in our home. He wore fine clothes but they were well worn. You could see the frayed threads in the seams and the dirt around the collar. I noticed his hands were smooth, not like the farm workers around these parts.

Late that night the stranger came into my room while I laid awake thinking about him. It was hot and my gown stuck to my body from the sweat and all. How he didn't look like the rest of the colored men around town. He was so handsome, blond hair with clear blue eyes. He was gentle and his touches put my body on fire. I couldn't resist his advances. I stayed very still and he rolled on top of my small body. He strolled into my life, and took what he wanted, and that was me.

The stranger spoke quietly holding me in his arms, "I'm going down to Galveston where it's beautiful and I can work as a gambler. I've heard there's a fortune just for the taking. If I make it rich, I'll come back for you. You're the prettiest thing I've ever seen. I promise."

The next morning Daddy and the stranger walked to fix his car. Daddy brought water and his tools. Daddy said the car was very low on water. He filled the water in the radiator and battery. Then he jumped the battery with cables from a passerby. Off it started. Surprised, the stranger didn't even offer him a ride back to town. Just waved off in the distance as he drove away. Daddy guessed he was in a hurry. Thought he would at least say, "Thank you" for all our hospitality.

The stranger never came back. My, how Daddy was mad when he found out I was having the strangers' child. He stomped and cursed until he could no more. He would have killed him if he knew where he had gone. My Mom just cried along aside me.

As I swished back and forth toward the library to study, the locals lined the streets just staring at us. I paid them no mind. The happy child smiled and waved as we passed each one. This was the highlight of her day.

One boy did not look at me as the others with judgement in their eyes. He was handsome, tall and strong. We had gone to school together until he quit to work in the fields. His father had a sun stroke and could not work anymore. His name was Louis Jackson; he had eight brothers and sisters to feed. His eyes were sad and I could tell he still wanted to talk with me as he had done on the playground at school. We would play tag and he chased me around. Sometimes, I would let him catch me. Those were happier times when we were young and innocent, not realizing our future. I was drawn to him, but he never spoke to me again after he quit school. I felt like we were the same, trapped into our responsibilities.

I studied at the library so I could use the encyclopedias as references in school work. My heart sank, looking at the people in the library who glared. They were old, their expressions possessed no spirit. I was so lonely. I wanted to keep my spirit and just do better. I had to finish high school. One day I would go down to Galveston and look for her Daddy. He had to be there. Maybe he was rich and could send me to a fine college and help with our daughter.

All my life I had studied hard and did well in school. I could have married anyone even at the age of thirteen when I met the stranger. I had a long line of suiters, but now at sixteen no one would have me since I had a child from a white man. They could make fun of me, but not my child. I guess that's why I started drinking tonic to forget the mistake of sleeping with a perfect stranger.

Mom suggested I go to the doctor who prescribed tonic for my depression after the baby was born. Soon I was addicted to the tonic. Sometimes I laid around all day and did absolutely nothing. I knew the tonic was a combination of heroin and opium, meant to help female ailments. Some days I got that faraway look as I sat in the chair waiting for the stranger to return. My daughter would often turn her head away from my gloomy, sunken eyes. I could see her confusion when I just stared into the darkness. She was just an innocent child.

After I finished my schoolwork, I left the library swishing back and forth toward home with my little girl. It was a late, hot, sultry night. Everyone had left the streets earlier in the evening before the library closed. No one was there to witness the sound of my starched slip and the harsh reality that I couldn't leave home for a better life. There was no one to take care of my Mom if I left town. She only had me as family since the Doc explained, "Daddy died of a broken heart."

I dreamed of being the first black woman in my town to go to college. I even fantasized that everyone would talk about how I succeeded in leaving this dusty town.

I slowly walked back home with my small child, swish, swish, back and forth into the empty streets silencing my cries into the night.

When I arrived home, I put my beloved child to bed. I sat in my chair staring into the darkness. I succumbed to the dreams of the stranger returning one day and taking us away from the small town. I wanted to leave this place forever and forget about my mistake, never forgiven by the town's people or my family. My fears and desires diminished into a world of numbness with each glass of tonic. Falling in a deep sleep, my last thoughts were of my child who was not a mistake but an innocent beautiful child.

Why I Wrote This Story

In the fifties, my father invited an African American man to come to our house to buy his boot legged beer while my mother was in the hospital. We had a big pot of beans and cornbread ready for supper. As a young child, I invited the man to dinner and he said, "I've never been in a white man's house nor invited to supper. Thank you, young lady for your kindness but I have to go home to my family." With those words, he left but I never forgot his words. I didn't understand as a child the magnitude of his words but now I do.

AUTHORS REVOLUTION

B Alan Bourgeois

THE CLOCK TICKED quickly down. I had less than an hour to read this book and it couldn't be done in that short period of time, but I had to finish reading it. The thrills, the chills, the mystery that this writer had created overwhelmed my senses. I should have known it was going to be this good. Why did I wait to read it? Now, down to the last day, the last hour, I had waited. When would I learn to stop procrastinating?

I stopped watching the clock and continued to read the fine craftsmanship the author used to create the characters, the fast pace of this thriller.

Caught up in the page-turning suspense of wanting, needing to know what was going to happen next. Ah, it would make a great film.

Time continued to tick away.

But, I had to read each word with careful consideration, as the author had clearly shown the story had unsuspecting twists. I stole a quick glance at the clock. Fifteen minutes left. Oh shit, I wasn't even halfway done!

"This is so f . . . ing unfair!" I yelled out. But it was fair and I knew it.

Forget about the clock. Keep reading. Get as much as I could out of it. I've read enough over the years, to be able to figure out 'who done it' by now. I wouldn't need to read the entire book.

"Shit!" I yelled, as the book toned the last five minutes left on the clock! No way was I going to figure out what would happen and who did it. The writer kept me hooked with all of the twists and turns. The new characters dropped in at just the right moment to add suspense and confusion. Damn, he was good.

"No," I scream to an empty room. Only I knew what was happening. Only I was to blame for not being able to finish reading the book in the time I had been given.

The books chimes rang. My time was up. Oh, I could pay the extra fee and continue to read, but I had already spent my allowance on books. No this was my fault. I thought I would have plenty of time to read it.

Life can just get in the way at times and now with these new laws and ways of reading books, I had no choice. Watch it disappear in front of me, or pay the extra fee to finish it.

Slowly, as the last bells rang, I set the book down on the coffee table. I had made the foolish mistake of holding a book in my hand once before as it evaporated into thin air. I was not going to go through the stinging in my hands again. No, I was not going to do that again.

The book disintegrated into thin air. Now I would not know who did it, or why, or anything that brought this masterpiece to an end.

As with so many things in our lives today, I chose to let this new system be created without voicing my objections and fighting for the old ways of life. But, I also understood why it was important that authors fought for this type of system. They clearly could not make a living without being properly compensated as their works were easily passed around and resold without earning them a single penny.

The many who fought against it said authors made their living from the first sale of the book and should not complain about earning royalties for resales, or lending of their works. But, I knew too many authors who could not make a living.

Their inability to do so caused a catechism of poorly written books or books that were ghost written about a famous reality TV star. In short, CRAP!

Few if any authors had the ability to have a spouse support them as they wrote. Or even worse, had the energy to write late at night once they had finished their grueling day jobs and taking care of their families once they got home. Those authors deserved a fighting chance, and they deserved the opportunities to create wonderful pieces of work.

Just like the man whose book had disintegrated on my coffee table. I could pay the extra couple of bucks to keep it longer or to re-purchase it for the ten days, or just wonder what did happen.

"Oh, screw it," I said once again to the empty living room and picked up my smartphone and logged into the book depository and ordered the book once again. IT was a good read, and well worth the five bucks to purchase.

Within seconds the book once again materialized on my coffee table.

Minutes, then a couple of hours quickly vanished as I continued to read this wonderful tale. It had me enthralled in such a way that one can only let time melt away. There is nothing like reading a great novel.

With the turn of the last page, I was pleasantly surprised at who had done it and how it ended. My hat's off to B Alan Bourgeois and his characters for once again delivering a great story for my enjoyment.

It was a shame that the author would not earn the royalties from his great works. But, I now know that authors of today and of the future can now earn a fair living through this new system. It is well worth it to have great stories come to life from a new breed on writers.

In the late 90's it was clear that a new revolution in the publishing world was beginning. While the changes have given authors more control, it really has not helped them in earning their fair share from book sales. I wrote this commentary to ignite the imagination of authors and to get support from readers of a new reality in how books are sold. Authors deserve to earn a fair share of income from their books, otherwise, we will lose quality writers as they are forced to work multiple jobs to pay the bills.

Why I Wrote This Story

In the late 90's it was clear that a new revolution in the publishing world was beginning. While the changes have given authors more control, it really has not helped them in earning their fair share from book sales. I wrote this commentary to ignite the imagination of authors and to get support from readers of a new reality in how books are sold. Authors deserve to earn a fair share of income from their books, otherwise, we will lose quality writers as they are forced to work multiple jobs to pay the bills.

RETURN TO SULPHUR RIVER

art anthony

2015
First Place
TEXAS
Western
Fiction

SULPHUR RIVER

art anthony

Available for speaking engagements at Libraries, Book clubs and Schools, etc.

2013

Art Loggings and Darrell Stroud became friends while serving in the Confederate Army. After returning home to Texas after the war, all they wanted was to be left alone to work their land and raise their families. However, they soon discover they have to survive punishment the Yankees gave the South because of the Civil War.

With lawlessness permeating Texas, follow these boys, as they become gunmen and fight against the villainous lawyer Lassiter, rustlers, and outlaws to help establish some type of lawful _____ for the people in the area. Even the Comanche and _____ destroy their farms and livestock as well as the farms _____ friends. But the Choctaw and ex-slaves become friends _____ them fight for survival.

RETURN TO SULPHUR RIVER

Art Anthony was born and raised in Goose Creek, Texas, and now resides in T_____ Oklahoma. He retired in 2012 after thirty-one years in education. Ten of those years he served as superintendent of the South Fork School District in Kincaid, Illinois. Before beginning his career, he spent two years in the army. His career began in agricultural manufacturing and marketing for twenty years. He is married with four children, six grandchildren, and three great-grandchildren. His passion is history and writing.

**104 Southpointe
Tuttle, Ok 73089
(405) 326-8077
Email: aanthony@pldi.net**

As the Civil War draws to a close, the desperate Confederate army drafts fifteen-year-old Art Logging in place of his dying father. *Sulphur River* follows Art and his friend Darrell Stroud through their service in the Red River campaign and into their journey to make men of themselves. Art's keen eye for business opportunities in the midst of a crumbling nation and Darrell's resourceful support could set both boys up for a comfortable life in Northeast Texas. If only it were that simple.

Art and Darrell aren't the only ones looking to take advantage of chaos in the South in the mid-1860s. They must navigate their cotton, cattle, and horses around Confederate deserters, a crooked lawyer, and their own passions to reach the markets where they are most likely to make a profit. The boys find natural allies among neighboring farmers and a few unnatural allies in escaped slaves, Indians, and even Union soldiers.

Author Art Anthony has loaded *Sulphur River* with research into the history, culture, and economics of the eastern edge of the Old West. Those interested in Civil War history or pioneer stories will especially appreciate the adventures of Art Logging.

LOCAL AUTHOR WINS AGAIN IN STATE WIDE BOOK CONTEST

Tuttle - We are pleased to announce Return to Sulphur River by Art D. Anthony has won 1st place in the Western Fiction category of the 2015 Texas Association of Authors book competition. Art's first book, Sulphur River, also won 1st place in the 2013 competition in the same Genre.

This is the fourth year for TxAuthors to select winning titles by Texas Authors. TxAuthors is currently accepting entries for books published during 2015. A sample chapter from each book can be found along with the previous year's winners at TxAuthors.com.

The winners from this year's contest will be presented at the State Capitol in Austin, Texas on April 11th at 11:00 a.m. As part of the DEAR Texas event on April 12th, they will be in an Austin book store doing a reading and book signing of all their books. For complete list of book stores that will be participating, please visit DearTexas.info.

Texas Association of Authors focuses on promoting authors. The association leverages the knowledge and expertise of various authors to promote their works locally and globally.

DISCOVERY - Poetry and Art
By Rick and Jan Sikes

Breaths of life from a prison cell
and beyond, with stunning
pen-and-ink drawings

Multi-Award Winning
Author, Jan Sikes
http://www.jansikes.com

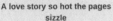

A love story so hot the pages
sizzle

When you've reached bottom,
there's only one way to go

Starting over with a pocket full
of dreams and heart full of love

Sand in the hourglass
grows thin and Luke fights
to leave a legacy.

BIOGRAPHICAL FICTION WITH A MUSICAL TWIST

After the Storm

Into each life some storms will come. Whether personal, such as divorce, or natural disaster such as Hurricane Harvey, recovery takes time.

Asunder follows Ellie through recovery after divorce in this page-turner novel. The accompanying study guide makes the book ideal for small group discussions and divorce recovery groups.

A Ready Hope is a fictional account of a natural disaster with very factual information about what to expect after the disaster when the response personnel arrive on the scene. Must reading for volunteers before they enter a disaster zone.

A portion of sales will be donated to a local disaster response agency in response to Hurricane Harvey.

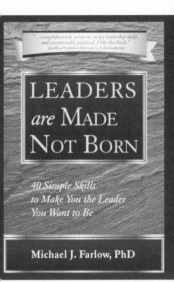

LEADERS
are MADE
NOT BORN
by Michael J. Farlow, PhD

LEADERSHIP SKILLS YOU NEED THAT WILL BRING
OUT THE BEST IN YOU AND MAKE YOU THE
LEADER YOU WANT TO BE . . .

AVAILABLE AT
MICHAELJFARLOW.COM

Anne Bonny's Wake
By Dick Elam

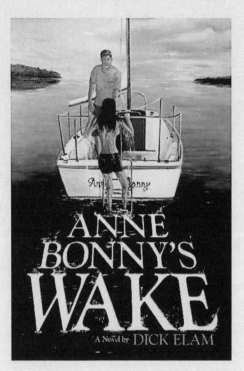

**Ahoy, Young Writers ...
and Readers, great....
"Come aboard "and
sail with me.**
This Old Salt published
my first novel at age 88. I
was a retired Professor
painting pictures until
my son read the
manuscript I abandoned
in the 1980's. "Hey, Old
Man, you paint a better
picture with words
than you do with paint.
Toss the brushes. Publish
this book."

   I stowed the brushes. Typed words to refloat our sailboat --- named after the female pirate, Anne Bonny, --- and launched my *"Dangerous Encounters on the Carolina Waterways"*.

   In Anne Bonny's wake, we are floating her audiobook, for Audible sale. In the book's wake, I have edited the sequel manuscript, "Guadalajara High". Also, editing manuscripts for books three and four in the series.

   More fun than when I wrote sports for a Texas daily newspaper. Or wrote editorials for the TV station I managed. Lots more fun than writing a university theses or dissertation. And when a reader says they enjoyed stowing away for voyages, that's the most fun of all.

Please find the books on **Amazon** or www.dickelambooks.com

Dick

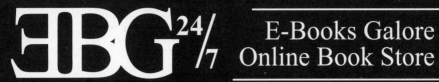

EBG 24/7
E-Books Galore
Online Book Store

Turn Your Creative Passion into Cash !

www.ebg247.com

 Authors Earn 80% Royalties

E-Books Galore pays 80% royalties, quarterly on all books sold. Our dashboard allows authors to view the amount of books sold as well as estimated royalties earned.

Check out our other services

- **Book Editing**
- **E Book File Conversion and Formatting**
- **Web Banner Design**
- **Custom Print Book Marks**
- **Hero Cards**

Visit us today at **http://www.ebg247.com/authors-services**

We Are Always Looking For New Authors.

Sign Up Today !

email:info@ebg247.com
www.facebook.com/ebg247

Texas Authors, Inc.

A not for profit organization that brings the Best of Texas to the World

Texas Association of Authors
The Only Non-Profit that Supports
& Markets Texas Authors
TxAuthors.com

DEAR Texas
A State Wide Book Festival
DearTexas.info

Lone Star Book Festival
Texas Largest Indy Book Festival
LoneStarBookFest.com

Texas Authors Institute of History
A Museum that Saves Texas Author History and Promotes
Education in Reading & Writing
TexasAuthors.Institute

gatekeeper press
Where Authors are Family

Developmental Editing & Proofreading	✓ Line Edit/Proofread — $10 per 1,000 words
	  • Spelling, grammar, punctuation, syntax, language-usage
	  • Recommendations for improving overall flow
	✓ Developmental Edit — $16 per 1,000 words
	  • Line edit plus sentence restructuring, focusing on consistency and style.
	    (e.g. abbreviations, numbers, hyphenations, etc.)
	  • Content and quality review, organization, transitions, tone, voice, complexity
	  • Fiction: plot holes and character inconsistencies, and suggestions as to dialogue,
	    pace, and clarity
	✓ Free Sample Edit, 1,000 Words

Cover Design	✓ $499 flat fee
	  • Three mock-up designs
	  • Two rounds of revisions
	  • Unlimited image/graphics
	  • Front cover, back cover and spine

Hardcover and Paperback Layout and Distribution	✓ $599 each (plus $1 per page for layout of all pages beyond 250)
	✓ 100% royalties, 100% rights, & 100% control
	✓ Free ISBN & front matter configuration
	✓ Unlimited images/graphics
	✓ Distribution virtually everywhere books are sold online worldwide
	  • Including brick and mortar option
	✓ POD and Offset Options — No minimum requirements
	  • No minimum purchase requirements
	✓ Drop shipping available
	✓ Case bound with or without dust jacket
	  • Foil Stamping on spine

eBook Layout, Conversion, & Distribution	✓ $299 flat fee
	  • No pre-formatting required
	  • Unlimited image/graphics
	  • Enhanced eBooks (audio/video) - no extra charges
	  • Fixed-layout eBooks - no extra charge
	  • For distribution across all platforms
	✓ 100% royalties, 100% rights, & 100% control
	✓ Free ISBN front matter configuration
	✓ Distribution virtually everywhere books are sold online worldwide

Illustrations	✓ $45 per illustration ✓ Can do any style ✓ Myriad Pro 

Exclusive Texas Authors coupon code:
TXAuthors10 for a 10% discount!
Schedule your FREE CONSULTATION at www.GatekeeperPress.com/tchellini